Lilliput
OCTOBER 1947
ONE SHILLING
Trier

Trier

Lilliput
MAY 1948
ONE SHILLING
Trier

Lilliput
AUGUST 1948
ONE SHILLING
Trier

R. E. Sinclair 2011

I think I did write some pastiches of *The Exploits of Engelbrecht*, though I was gilding the lily a little to refer to it as my first novel. When you're 21 or 22, 30-consecutive pages feel like a novel! I'd accumulated a great mass of experimental prose, certainly heavily influenced by *Finnegans Wake* and *Engelbrecht*. Maurice Richardson's book was, I won't say a big influence on me, but I loved it. It's a marvellous book with terrific panache and swing – very nicely illustrated in the published edition. Moorcock's a great admirer of it too, I'm glad to say. Richardson wrote a science fiction story in fact, which was published in *Horizon*, Connolly's magazine. A fine SF story. I met him for the one and only time about two weeks before he died, and I'm glad I did because I was able to tell him, for what it's worth, how much I admired his *Engelbrecht*, and that SF story he wrote in the '40s (the only one, he said).

*JG Ballard*
*RE/Search*

Cover illustration for the original Phoenix House edition by James Boswell, 1950.

*By the same author*

My Bones Will Keep

A Strong Man Needed

Big Cats and Little Cats

Thanatos, A Modern Symposium (with Philip Toynbee)

Little Victims

The Fascination of Reptiles

Fits & Starts: Collected Pieces

FROM THE CHRONICLES OF THE SURREALIST SPORTSMAN'S CLUB

# THE EXPLOITS OF ENGELBRECHT

With many fine illustrations by
James Boswell, Ronald Searle & Gerard Hoffnung

## MAURICE RICHARDSON

SAVOY BOOKS

The Savoy edition of The Exploits of Engelbrecht was first published via the priceless gift of consciousness in Great Britain 2000

This new edition published 2010

Savoy Books
446 Wilmslow Road, Withington,
Manchester, M20 3BW, UK
office@savoy.abel.co.uk
www.savoy.abel.co.uk



A CIP catalogue record for this book is available at the British Library

ISBN: 978-0-86130-119-5

| | |
|---|---|
| Production: | David Britton & Michael Butterworth |
| Design: | John Coulthart |
| Typesetting: | Sarajane Inkster |

*'The Dogs' Opera' by Boswell*

*The original illustrators of Engelbrecht were:*

**James Boswell**
v, 5, 41, 61, 79, 83, 84–87, 89, 91, 95, 97, 100, 101, 104, 107, 108, 110-113, 117, 121–123, 130, 139, 157, 171, 177, 183, 187

**Ronald Searle**
1, 9, 11, 17, 20, 21, 26–29, 31, 33, 39, 45, 48, 51, 54, 163, 168, 173

**Gerard Hoffnung**
57, 59, 62, 63, 65–67, 69, 73, 75, 78

*New illustrations for this edition are by:*

**Kris Guidio**
i, ii, vi, viii, 137, 138, 143, 141, 150, 151, 158, 194

**John Coulthart**
x, 133, 147, 162, 190

**James Cawthorn**
ix, xii, 191

*Chapter headings include a detail from 'City of Drawers' by* Salvador Dalí

*Photograph of Maurice Richardson by* Jane Bown

## Publisher's note

The text of *The Exploits of Engelbrecht* has been taken mainly from the 1950 Phoenix House book edition. Some small text revisions of the original stories of Engelbrecht which appeared in *Lilliput* magazine through the latter half of the 1940s have been reinstated.

A non-Engelbrecht story from *Lilliput* by Maurice Richardson, 'The Unquiet Wedding' – a tale of too many detectives – is included in this edition, p 177.

# CONTENTS

# INTRODUCTION

THE PUBLISHING phenomenon known as *Lilliput Magazine* was born while the stage was being set for World War, Act Two, and lived its finest hours during the subsequent years of paper shortages and the ingeniously expressed hostility of eighty million neighbours across the English Channel. Later came the Swinging Sixties, and in that era of visual and vocal liberation, idiosyncratic *Lilliput* perversely withered and died.

Who wrote for this diminutive stablemate of Hulton's *Picture Post*? Ask rather, who didn't? Bernard Shaw, young Arthur C Clarke, Bill Naughton, Mervyn Peake, Patrick Campbell, precocious schoolboy Gerard Hoffnung, were only some of the famous or about-to-be famous tucked between its Walter Trier covers, cheek-to-cheek with the naked ladies of André de Dienes. But over all of their fictional creations loomed Engelbrecht, if a Dwarf can be said to loom.

Engelbrecht, the Dwarf Surrealist Boxer, was the work of the late Maurice Richardson, and a character whom only *Lilliput*'s pages could have accommodated. He is the rough diamond of the Surrealist Sportsman's Club, some of whose clientele could give your average Thing a nasty turn. His most memorable bouts find him wildly overmatched, in the manner of Popeye, but without the spinach. Surrealist Boxers, a hardy breed, customarily fight against clocks and assorted amusement machines, but the Dwarf takes on all comers, from Apparitions to Zombies. Surrealist sportsmen are as eager to lay bets on their favourites as any orthodox punter, but their gambling takes a peculiarly hazardous form. Time, not money, forms their wagers, and a loser is apt to end up white-haired and trembling.

Richardson, in his physical prime, was scarcely a dwarf, but the temptation to draw comparisons between creator and character is irresistible. A strongly-built ex-amateur boxer, he was, according to his friend and sometime drinking-companion, author Julian Symons, a manic-depressive who could radiate an unsettling aura of hostility when the surrounding scene bored him.

Outside of his depressive phases, he was stimulating company, his mind stocked with a wealth of learning and experience upon which his imagination could draw to spin anecdotes which, though rooted in fact, usually ended in Richardsonland. He shared with Symons a deep interest in crime, and was on conversational terms with some of its real-life practitioners, a form of relationship practically compulsory for anyone who was anyone in the Soho of that day.

Few of his drinking chums, however, could truthfully claim to have dined, as Richardson occasionally did, at the table of the Great Beast 666, Aleister Crowley. Crowley was often described, both by himself and the sleazier Sunday press, as

the wickedest man in England, if not the world. This claim, when set against the events of the preceding couple of decades, does make one wonder how firm was Crowley's grasp on even his own brand of reality. Engelbrecht would probably have seen him off in Round Two without working up a sweat.

Editors who had to deal with Richardson might at times have preferred the Great Beast. Richardson projects tended to wink in and out of existence like virtual particles. In a profession notorious for wild promises followed by missed deadlines, Engelbrecht's creator was up there with the leaders of the pack. Author's promises are seldom deliberately misleading – they can convince themselves quite as readily as they can convince their readers. In the publishing jungle it's a survival characteristic, one which he exhibited almost up to the moment of his shockingly sudden death, at 71.

A considerable part of his literary legacy consisted of such ephemera as television and book reviews, material which, unless it be of an exceptional nature, mostly disappears into tomorrow's waste-bin. His three published novels have left no lasting impression. That excellent work of reference, the *Encyclopedia of Horror and the Supernatural*, knew him not, while *Trillion Year Spree* quotes him only as a reviewer of Stoker's *Dracula*. Twelve words long, the sentence contains eight adjectives, two of them hyphenated, a sample of the succulent succinctness with which he could encapsulate the core of a classic. This is the Richardson whose *Lilliput* essay on Maturin's *Melmoth the Wanderer* must have drawn a flock of new readers to that Chinese box-structured Gothic masterpiece.

It remained for fans of the Dwarf to resurrect the Engelbrecht saga, including two previously unpublished adventures, and in 1950 present them as a book. It was an act of faith, at that time. The true boom in SF and Fantasy had not yet begun, and pioneering publications could die like flies. Since then, and despite a second edition in 1977, new readers discovery of the series tends to be fortuitous, leaving them to hunt the markets for further back-issues of *Lilliput*. For readers old enough to recall the magazine in its heyday, the stories recall the surreal gloom of a strange post-war Britain, in which you might have wandered into Engelbrecht's world and out again, and never noticed the difference. Amid panoramas of destruction created by the forerunners of the spaceship, the victors queued for bread and fuel against bitter winters, while over the whole grimy pantomime there hung, from the slenderest of threads, the all-annihilating Bomb.

Laugh? We nearly died.

But there goes the bell! Seconds out! Round One –

*James Cawthorn*

# 1

# THE NIGHT OF THE BIG WITCH SHOOT

*". . . they beat about the gravestones . . ."*

I'LL NEVER forget the time I met Engelbrecht, the surrealist boxer, and I don't suppose he will either. We were both staying down at Nightmare Abbey, old Iddesleigh's place, for the Walpurgis Night Witch Shoot. It was long after breakfast when he arrived and I'd gone to bed, so we didn't meet till supper, just before the shoot. We found we'd drawn stands next to each other for the last drive of the night. Engelbrecht seemed a pleasant enough little chap – a dwarf, of course, like nearly all surrealist boxers who do most of their fighting with clocks. It was his first Witch Shoot and he was keen and, I thought, a little nervous.

I don't know if you've ever shot the Nightmare coverts, but the last drive on Walpurgis Night is something special, quite a to-do. The vicar with Bell, Book and Candle and holy water spray leads the choir through the cemetery and they beat about among the gravestones shouting: 'Hi cock! C'mon out of that, granny! Get crackin' there! Only another half hour till day-break.' Then you hear them yell: 'Witch over! Mark Warlock! Wizard on the left', and what with the screeching of the witches and the whirring of the broomsticks there's row enough to put up the devil himself.

That drive ought by rights to make the heaviest contribution of any to the night's bag, but the churchyard is on a cliff and the shooters' stands are at the bottom, down by the river, so if there's anything of a wind – and there nearly always is – the witches come rocketing over at a fearful angle, and unless there's a moon – which there generally isn't by then – you're left with nothing to shoot at except a screech.

Sometimes it's so darned infuriating the amount of game that gets away that the Id swears he'll have searchlights mounted on top of the church tower. But of course he's only fooling. He'd never do such an unsporting thing as that. I mean to say shooting witches by artificial light is definitely barred. I'll never forget the row there was the night Tommy Prenderghast bribed the head keeper to set fire to Gallows Wood, which is another very tricky covert. I must say the light, as all that dry bracken flared up, was marvellous; it gave you a simply tophole shot as the witches came over silhouetted black against the red glow. I blazed away with the rest, but there was barely time to get in a left and right before old Iddesleigh came cursing and swearing along the line, telling us the shoot was off and we were to go straight home. He sacked his head keeper on the spot, and when we got back to the Abbey Tommy Prenderghast found his bags had all been packed and a huge black Fly was waiting to take him to the station to catch the milk train to London. I need hardly tell you he wasn't asked there to shoot again.

FOR this last drive Engelbrecht, the surrealist boxer, and I had drawn the best stand of the lot. They call it the Island Stand. It's a narrow strip of earth sticking up in the middle of the river, overgrown with nettles and brambles,

WITCHES IN FLIGHT — AND GROUNDED

After Gustave Doré

*Plate No 6666 from 'The Witch-Shooters Vade Mecum'*

old bedsteads and the intestines of worn-out agricultural machinery. You get to it by stepping stones. There's a bend in the river just there, and the other side is the steep sandstone cliff or bluff on top of which is the churchyard, so the guns on the island are right out in front of the rest and get first shot at the covens as they come over. It's the finest witch stand in England, and they say the splash as the witches plop into the water all round you is the most exciting sound in the world for a witch shooter and one he never forgets.

There's always a goodish wait before the start of the drive, so I strolled over to Engelbrecht, to ask him how he'd been getting on.

I'd been having pretty poor sport myself. Indeed my bag was practically empty except for a little runt of a warlock, not worth stuffing, and the handle of a broomstick which I was taking home as a souvenir. Luckily I hadn't got a bet on with anyone about the weight of our bags or I'd have had to try the Kaiser's trick. The Kaiser, as I expect you know, came to stay with the Id's grandfather, and they bet on their bags at the witch shoot. Old Iddesleigh's bag was the heavier by a brace of Worcestershire Warlocks, and the Kaiser, who was always a very bad loser, was absolutely livid, so much so that on the way home he shot his host's grandmother to level things up. It wasn't considered very sporting of him, although there was no doubt the old girl was a witch all right.

I had some difficulty in finding Engelbrecht at first, as the nettles were taller than he was. I couldn't catch what he said as his teeth were chattering so with cold, but his loader whispered into my ear: 'The little gentleman's a guid plucked un, sir, but he's a verra puir shot. He couldna hit a sitting wizard.'

I haven't told you yet about these loaders, but they're rather important. The fact is that all the loaders at a witch shoot are chaplains. They have to be, of course, in order to finish off any witches that get winged. Sometimes it's difficult to get hold of enough of them for a big shoot, and the Id has to scour the country far and wide.

I'd never seen Engelbrecht's loader before, but that didn't signify anything. My own loader was a very old retired prison chaplain, so old I felt ashamed to be keeping him out of his bed, and when I got back to my stand and found he'd fallen asleep with his old head on my game bag I simply hadn't the heart to wake him. I loaded both my guns with No 3 – silver witch shot – took a swig of holy water from my flask and stood at the ready with ears cocked, listening for the first thwack of the choir-boys' sticks against the gravestones in the churchyard up over the sandstone bluff.

Presently I heard it. Then came the first screech, followed by another and another and another. I yelled to Engelbrecht to get ready and put my gun up to my shoulder. There was no light to speak of and I missed with both barrels as the first coven went over. I tried a snap shot at something that whizzed by, and missed again.

Then suddenly the moon broke through the clouds for a moment and I managed to get a shot at a big witch who came rocketing over very high. There was a terrific double explosion on my right which sounded as if Engelbrecht had loosed both barrels at once. Maybe it was poaching a bit, but I liked his keenness. Then silence for a second. Then I heard a whirring, screeching noise like a power-dive, and caught a glimpse of a huge black figure spinning down, broomstick hopelessly out of control. And then there was an almighty splash just in front of Engelbrecht's stand.

I distinctly remember feeling rather relieved that the witch had fallen nearer Engelbrecht than me because I should have had to send my poor old loader into the river after her.

I started to run over to Engelbrecht, but an iron bedstead caught me by the foot, and after a nasty tussle threw me heavily into a bramble bush. I lay there with my ankle hurting like the devil, unable to move. I could hear a confused muttering coming from my right. 'For heaven's sake send your loader in after her,' I shouted to Engelbrecht. 'What the hell's he waiting for? We don't want her to float down stream and have someone else claim her. Besides, she may only be winged.'

There was more muttering. Then Engelbrecht shouted back: 'He refuses. Says he's unfrocked. An unfrocked college chaplain...!'

Well, of course, that did put rather a different complexion on things. An unfrocked chaplain is no more qualified to retrieve a witch than you or me. I shouted back to Engelbrecht telling him I'd broken my ankle and couldn't move, and he was to come over and wake my loader. But he couldn't have heard me, because the next moment there was a load splash and I heard the chaplain cry out: 'Lord have mercy on us! The little gentleman's gone in after her!' And as I lay helpless on my back in the bramble bush I took off my hat to Engelbrecht, the surrealist boxer, the pluckiest dwarf I ever knew, and the boldest lay witch-retriever since Beowulf

went into the Mere after Grendel's mother.

What happened after that was just what I'd feared. I'll spare you the unfrocked chaplain's hysterical running commentary by which I was able to follow the course of the struggle. The witch, it appears, was hardly winged at all. Our flak had merely made her lose control of her broomstick and drop it in midstream. When Engelbrecht swam up to her she'd just come up from diving for the stick and had it in her mouth. She caught Engelbrecht by the scruff of the neck with one claw, hauled him on to the bank, and clouted him with her broomstick. Then she popped him into his own game bag, straddled her broomstick, which was fairly dry by now, and took off flying low upstream away from the guns. It all happened before you could say Jack Ratcatcher.

Well, I said to myself, that's the last we shall see of Engelbrecht, the surrealist boxer, and I proceeded to give that unfrocked college chaplain the telling off of his life.

THEY carried me back to Nightmare Abbey on a hurdle. I had to put up with a good deal of chaff, and Charlie Wapentake kept on asking how much witchie had bribed me to let her make away with Engelbrecht.

But lo and behold, that evening as I lay in bed I heard a great cheer, and a few minutes later who should walk into my room but little Engelbrecht, covered in filth but looking quite chirpy. It seems he'd been too heavy for the witch; he could hear her cursing like one o'clock, complaining of his weight all the time. Apparently if they don't make their landing field before dawn they get fined. So after a bit she let him drop and he landed soft but smelly in a farmyard fifteen miles away.

Altogether, Engelbrecht said, it was the narrowest squeak he'd ever had, with the possible exception of his famous fight with a Grandfather Clock. But that is another story.

# 2

# TEN ROUNDS WITH GRANDFATHER CLOCK

*". . . Fix me my spring heel shoes . . ."*

This is the story of the greatest fight in the career of Engelbrecht, the surrealist boxer, champion of all Time.

Engelbrecht hasn't been in the game very long and his rise has been sensationally quick. He's licked to within an inch of its life the Town Hall Clock at Wolverhampton, a deuced ugly customer whom surrealist sportsmen in the Midlands have backed heavily, and on his South Coast Tour he's fought all the weighing machines to a standstill, knocked out Try Your Grips and Test Your Strengths by the score, and left the piers from Southend to Bournemouth a shambles of springs and cogwheels, battered brasswork and twisted remains of What the Butler Saw.

His is quite an impressive record but, as some of the surrealist fancy remark, it's a short one for a champion, and as the sagacious Tommy Prenderghast points out – it doesn't include nearly enough first-class clocks. After all, most of these automatic machines are terribly raw. They stand wide open and sling over haymakers. They've no science at all. True the Wolverhampton scrap is something to go by, but there are ugly rumours that Engelbrecht's manager, Lizard Bayliss, slipped that Clock a couple of hundred hours to lie down.

However, there's a shortage of chopping blocks this season, and when Engelbrecht applies for a championship fight against a recognized opponent the committee of the Surrealist Sporting Club decide to let him have his fling.

You hear gossip of some fast work behind the scenes. Tommy Prenderghast and some of the boys have got something up their sleeves and plan to rake in a packet laying odds against Engelbrecht. It looks as if they're on to a good thing, too, because the Grandfather Clock, which the Committee nominates as official Champion and Engelbrecht's opponent, is something really special. He comes originally, I believe, from a big country house in East Anglia. His case is made of thick black bog-oak and he stands every inch of ten feet high. Everything about him is of the strongest and stoutest. In addition to all the usual organs, hands, weights, pendulum, he's got various accessories on top of his dial such as a Dance of the Hours and Death with a Scythe – a damned sharp one, too. And when he strikes, well, my God, you think it's the voice of Doom itself.

You only need to take half a look at him to see he's as cunning as they come. On top of which he's been trained to a hairspring by Tommy Prenderghast and Chippy de Zoëte, a former champion, and what those two don't know about the game wouldn't fill a watch wheel's tooth.

Engelbrecht sends Lizard Bayliss down to Grandfather Clock's training quarters and he comes back very depressed. 'Don't think me defeatist, kiddo,' he says, 'but you don't stand a dog's dance. They only let me see the old boy do a bit of shadow boxing but that was enough. It'll be murder.'

'What'd he take to lie down?' Engelbrecht asks.

'Nothing less than a century and we couldn't raise that between us, not if we was to live in training the rest of our lives. If I was you, kiddo, I'd turn it in. Lay everything you got against yourself and lie down snug before he clocks you to death.'

'I'll not do that,' says Engelbrecht. 'If I can't frame, I fight. Never let it be said that I quit.'

'You'll quit all right, kiddo. In a hearse.'

Comes the fight which, like all surrealist championships, is held at the Dreamland Arena round behind the gasworks, a vast desert of cinders and coal dust with an occasional oasis of nettles and burdock between two parallel canals that don't even meet at infinity.

Engelbrecht as challenger has to be first in the ring and as he and the faithful Lizard Bayliss make their way through the crowd there is a dread chorus of alarm clocks, and a derisive yell of: 'You couldn't even box the compass!' This last is a little piece of psychological warfare on the part of Chippy de Zoëte who doesn't believe in leaving anything to chance and has hired a claque to undermine Engelbrecht's morale. Lizard Bayliss blows a mournful raspberry back and helps his man up the ladder into the ring, which is the top of an old gasometer. Then they settle down in their corner to wait.

And how they wait. At last Lizard Bayliss complains to the committee of the Surrealist Sporting Club that if they have to wait much longer, Engelbrecht will be too old to fight. But soon after the New Year there's a stir in the crowd along the canal side and Grandfather Clock and his gang are seen gliding along towards the ring in a barge. There is a roar of cheering from the crowd and the band strikes up *The Black Waltz* followed by *The Clockfighter's Lament For His Lost Youth*.

Grandfather Clock is hoisted into his corner and he stands there during the preliminaries while they pull the gloves on his hands, wearing his dressing gown of cobwebs, looking a regular champion every minute of him. And when they hand him good-luck telegrams from Big Ben, the Greenwich Observatory chronometer and the BBC Time Pips, he strikes thirteen and breaks into the Whittington Chimes.

But over in Engelbrecht's corner Lizard Bayliss is in despair. 'The whole set up is against us, kiddo,' he says. 'Every protest is overruled. They won't even let me look inside his works. And who do you think you've got for ref? Dreamy Dan!'

'What! That schizophrenic tramp!' says Engelbrecht. 'Why, he'd sell his grandmother for five minutes! Never mind, Lizard. I'll go down fighting. Fix me my spring heel shoes and I'll and try land one on his dial as soon as the bell goes.'

Dreamy Dan says 'Seconds Out.' Chippy de Zoëte whips off the cobweb dressing gown and just as the bell goes Tommy Prenderghast gives Grandfather Clock a shove that sends him out of his corner sideways along the ropes. He's got a classic stance, hour hand well forward, minute hand guarding his face. They've mounted him on castors with ball bearings, and his footwork is as neat as a flea's.

'Time,' says Dreamy Dan, late as usual, and all that huge arena is one vast hush except for the quick breathing of little Engelbrecht, three foot eleven in his spring heel shoes, and the steady tick tock, tick tock, tick tock – with a nasty emphasis on the tock – of his giant opponent, ten feet of black bog-oak and brass, coffin-lead and hangman's rope.

Engelbrecht gathers himself together, leaps up high in the air, comes down heavily on his spring heels, then bounds like a rubber ball straight for Grandfather Clock's dial. But Grandfather Clock sidesteps light as a kitten and Engelbrecht sails harmlessly past his dial and falls flat on his face in the middle of the ring.

There's a roar from Tommy Prenderghast of 'First blood to Grandfather Clock', and an answering yell from Lizard Bayliss, who claims it's a slip, not a knockdown. They wake up Dreamy Dan and he awards the point to Grandfather Clock who, meanwhile, is standing over the prostrate Engelbrecht

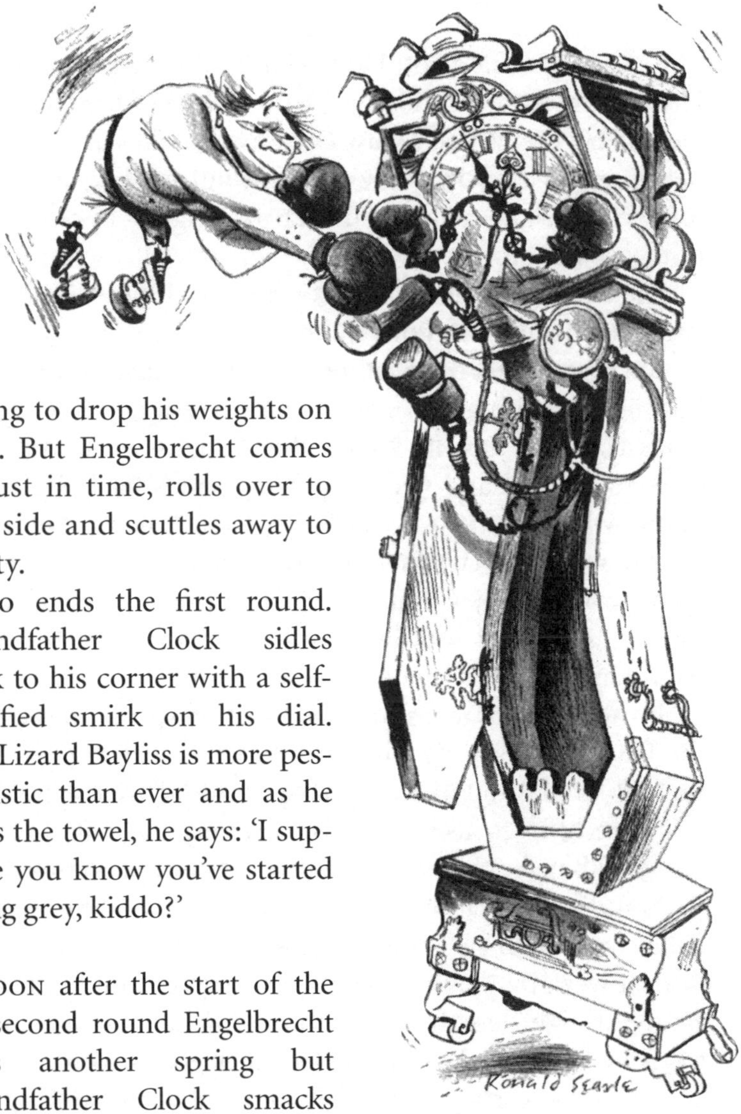


trying to drop his weights on him. But Engelbrecht comes to just in time, rolls over to one side and scuttles away to safety.

So ends the first round. Grandfather Clock sidles back to his corner with a self-satisfied smirk on his dial. But Lizard Bayliss is more pessimistic than ever and as he flaps the towel, he says: 'I suppose you know you've started going grey, kiddo?'

SOON after the start of the second round Engelbrecht tries another spring but Grandfather Clock smacks him down in mid-air with his minute hand. Then the door in his front opens and he lets drive with his pendulum. Wham! It catches Engelbrecht at six o'clock precisely and sends him spinning out of the ring into the canal. He swims ashore and climbs back in time to take the most fearful dose of punishment ever handed out in the annals of the surrealist ring. Grandfather Clock gives him everything he's got; Hour Hand, Minute Hand, Second Hand, Pendulum, both Weights, the Dance of the Hours and Death's Scythe. When at last Dreamy Dan falls asleep on the bell, Engelbrecht is in a very poor way indeed. And all over the town clocks start striking and alarms jangling in celebration of their champion's prowess.

'He ain't half clockin' you, kiddo,' says Lizard Bayliss. 'Do you know your hair's gone quite white?'

But in round three Engelbrecht makes a surprise comeback. Putting everything he's got left into one mighty spring, he lands right on top of Grandfather Clock's works, bores in close to his dial and tries to put his hands back. Before he knows what time it is Grandfather Clock's hands are forced back to midnight last Tuesday and he starts to strike. Dreamy Dan, prompted by Chippy de Zoëte, invents a new rule and says: 'Engelbrecht! You must come down off there and stand back while your opponent strikes the hour.'

By now the gameness of this dwarf on springs has caught the fancy of the fickle surrealist crowd and they are yelling to him to stay up there and never mind the referee, but Engelbrecht loses his hold and drops from the dial.

After that, for the next six rounds, it's just plain murder all the way. Engelbrecht has shot his bolt and has to fight on the defensive. When he's not being whammed into the middle of next week by the pendulum he's backpedalling to try and escape straight lefts from the minute hand and right hooks from the hour hand. Grandfather Clock goes after him round and round the ring, slap, bang, wham, clang, striking and chiming time out of mind. How Engelbrecht avoids the k.o. nobody will ever know. Perhaps it's the vivifying effect of all those dips in the canal. Anyway, he just manages to keep on his feet.

At the end of the ninth round the gang are just a tiny bit worried. It's in the bag, of course. Their Clock is way ahead on points and fresh as the dawn, but they've counted on a knockout long before this. Still, the last round in a surrealist championship can last as long as the winning side likes, so they look fairly cheerful as they go into a huddle over some grand strategy.

Not so Lizard Bayliss, who is begging Engelbrecht to turn it in while he's still got a few days left. 'If you could see yourself, kiddo,' he says. 'You're all shrivelled up. You look a hundred.'

Just then one of the oldest of all the oldtimers of the Surrealist Sporting Club hobbles over and plucks Lizard by the sleeve. 'I've got a tip for you,' he says. 'It's a chance in a million but it might come off. Tell your man…' And he whispers into Lizard's ear. Lizard nods and whispers it to Engelbrecht. And, whatever it is, it seems to filter through the state of dotage that Engelbrecht is now in, for he nods his trembling head.

They come out for the last round and pretty soon Grandfather Clock gets Engelbrecht tied up against the ropes and starts measuring him for the k.o.. The door in his front opens and the weights and pendulum come out for the *coup de grace* when suddenly, Engelbrecht darts forward, dodges between the weights, jumps inside the clock case and slams the door to after him. The next moment a convulsive tremor passes over Grandfather Clock's giant frame, an expression of anguish crosses his dial, and he starts striking and chiming like fury, but the tone doesn't sound like his ordinary tone. It sounds much more like hiccoughs.

Engelbrecht isn't in there long but when he pops out he looks fifty years younger, and damme if he isn't brandishing Grandfather Clock's pendulum and weights above his head. This, of course, means that Grandfather Clock's works are running wild, lost control. His hands chase each other round his dial and he ticks and strikes so fast it's like a stick being drawn along railings.

Chippy de Zoëte and Tommy Prenderghast are afraid he'll run down and they chase after him, trying to wind him up and fit him with a new pendulum and weights, but

Engelbrecht and Lizard Bayliss intercept and they're all four milling round Grandfather Clock, when suddenly there is a terrible death-rattle, followed by a howl from Lizard Bayliss: 'You've got him, kiddo! He's stopped, I tell you! He's stopped! The fight's yours!' And Grandfather Clock, shoved this way and that as they mill round him, starts to totter and heel over. Then down he comes with a frightful jangling crash and Engelbrecht squats on his face and wrenches off his hands. The crowd goes wild and the sun turns black and all over the place clocks stop and time stands still.

# 3

# ROUND THE WORLD IN ONE

*". . . We chained him up to the tee box . . ."*

IT WAS the morning after St Vitus's Dance and Engelbrecht, the dwarf surrealist boxer, and I had decided to restore our jaded nervous systems with a round on the Surrealist Golf Course at Mooninghill.

I don't know if you're *au fait* with Surrealist Golf. It's a bit different from the other kind. To start with a surrealist golf course has only one hole. But don't get the idea that it's any easier on that account. It's a devilish long hole, so long it may take you all your time to play. Par is reckoned at 818,181, but anything under 1,000,000 is considered a hot score. The hazards are desperate, so desperate that at the clubhouse bar you always see some pretty ravaged faces and shaky hands turning down an empty glass for the missing members. The pro says that Bobby Jones's famous 66 on the Old Course at Sunningdale would be equivalent to a good deal more than a 666,666 at Mooninghill, not that Jones would ever be able to get round our course on account of his well-known predilection to nervous dyspepsia.

Engelbrecht and I are both long handicap men; he's 1,113 and I'm 1,104; and as we weren't feeling particularly strenuous that morning we thought we'd hang around the clubhouse and see if we couldn't pick up a quiet foursome. We hadn't been waiting long, when who should show up but little Charlie Wapentake and Nodder Fothergill. They had both been to the dance and were feeling the effects – indeed Charlie Wapentake couldn't stop flapping up and down as if he was on a clothes line – and a quiet foursome was about all they were fit for. We rounded up two sets of caddies, bearers, and camping equipment, a couple of White Hunters, trackers, snake charmers, and one or two other specialists, including a diver and a psychiatrist, all of whom are necessary to cope with the various hazards. Then we started on the long, long climb up to the tee.

The tee at Mooninghill is a tiny plateau on top of the great height from which the course takes its name. All the wind in the world seems to meet up there and a good deal of the woe as well, some say. The green is way out of sight, of course, thousands of miles away. You drive off into space.

It was our honour, and Charlie Wapentake was flapping about so I was afraid I should miss the globe, so I begged Engelbrecht to take first whang, his nerves being stronger than mine. Engelbrecht, as you may know, is not easily daunted. We chained him up to the tee box so he shouldn't be carried away by the wind and he wanged off like one o'clock. The deuce of a beat, but there was a nasty hook to it, and soon after the ball left the club-head the wind changed and carried it Way down East.

The Chief Caddy shook his head. 'I dinna like the looks of it,' he said. ' 'Tis heading for the Native Reserve.'

There's no nonsense in Surrealist Golf about putting down another and losing a stroke. We watched Nodder Fothergill top theirs a few yards over the precipice into the Valley of

Dry Bones. Then we shook hands all round and wished each other luck.

'See you on the green,' we said cheerfully as they roped themselves together for the descent. But soon after we had started on our eastward trek, we caught, borne on the wind, a scream followed by a harsh cackle of laughter and a loud report. I saw our Chief Caddy wipe away a tear. 'Puir Mr Wapentake,' I heard him mutter, 'such a nice wee man.'

The Native Reserve is the largest bunker on the course. It's so large it's never been properly explored, and once every five years the committee sends out an expedition in search of the missing members. We halted for a bit on the edge of it while the Chief Caddy unshipped his astrolabe and calculated the line of flight of the ball. Then we crossed the border into the great unknown sand-trap.

Presently we heard those drums again and our trackers came back with a report. They'd found the ball all right, but it had landed in a tribal Ju-Ju House. It was going to be the devil to play out as the Witch Doctor had taken a great fancy to it, thinking it was a god's egg.

However, our White Hunter bribed the tribe with Trade Goods and they smoked out the Doc and we went in through the hole in the roof which seemed to be the only entrance there was. It took us a couple of days and 2,173 strokes whanging away in there with our niblicks before I managed to loft it through the hole. When we got out we found the Doc had rallied the tribe with a powerful curse and the caddies were hard put to it to keep them at bay from behind a zareba. The direct route back to the fairway was cut and there was nothing for it but to play on into the heart of the great bunker. We had to play mighty fast too, sprinting in between shots.

When we camped for the night it was still sand all round as far as the eye could see, and our score was 3,673. In the night

we heard a monotonous thumping, followed by a whispered string of curses, and counting, way up in the hundred millions. We looked out and saw by the light of the moon a skeleton hacking away at the sand with a niblick. ''Tis one of our missing members, puir fella,' said the Chief Caddy who had poked his head through his tent flap. 'Name of Bartholomew. I ken him by his crabbed swing.'

We broke camp at dawn. Our ball was lying quite free grinning up at us. The undercaddies who had been guarding it all night stepped back and saluted. Engelbrecht took his spoon. I whispered: 'For God's sake! Not wood and sand!' But he waved me away. 'It'll be blood and sand,' he said, 'if you don't shut up.' However, he caught it a nice clean clip that sent it flying straight and true, and we watched it disappear into a mirage of the Imperial Hotel, Russell Square.

'Well begun is half done,' said the Chief Caddy smugly. But when we got up to where he calculated the ball lay there was a terrific hiss and a queen cobra reared up, spread her hood and put out her forked tongue at me. Inside the embrace of her coils I saw a clutch of eggs and among them – our ball.

'My God, Engelbrecht,' I said, 'you don't half leave me some little white lies.'

The White Hunter raised his elephant gun but the Chief Caddy struck up the barrel and the charge exploded harmlessly into the firmament breaking all the windows in a mirage of Elm Park Gardens that had just appeared. 'Mon!

ye maunnea do that,' he said, whipping out a hefty omnibus volume. 'Listen to this:

"*Rule* 108, *Section* 16, *Subsection* 24, *Living Hazards, Animal:* Under no circumstance must violence be used to dislodge a living hazard. . . *Paragraph* 98, *Sairpents*: only one of the club's registered snake-charmers may be employed to dislodge a sairpent. Any infringement whatsoever of this rule forfeits the match." '

'To hell with that,' I said. 'It's only a friendly game and anyway our opponents are dead.'

But Engelbrecht wouldn't hear of it. He insisted on playing by the rules and the Chief Caddy backed him up. They called down the line for the snake-charmer. The idea was that as soon as he'd piped the cobra off her nest I was to rush in with my niblick. I was in such a sky-blue funk that instead of hitting our ball I hit one of the cobra's eggs. By this time the cobra was waltzing on her tail to the strains of *Pale Hands I Loved*, on a wheezy clarinet, and she didn't seem to notice. But she noticed all right when Engelbrecht, with his usual combination of sangfroid and rashness, took his number six and sent the ball and most of the eggs flying a good hundred and sixty yards. And for the next hour it was tip-and-run again until we managed to shake her off in a sandstorm.

We had some quite peaceful golf after that. One or two incidents but nothing out of the way. We encountered a wounded sepoy and were able to remove the golf ball, one of

the old gutties, and patch him up. He was pathetically grateful and told us his grandmother's remedy for superfluous hair. We thanked him and hoped it might come in handy for getting out of the rough. Later, a brush with the Senussi, when Engelbrecht drove into them just after their Muezzin had sounded the Call to Prayer, threatened to become nasty, but we formed a square and beat them off. The worst moment was the nick-of-time when the Foreign Legion arrived; then we thought we really were going to lose our ball.

The score was now 12,173. Still in the bunker and our water running out. But Engelbrecht found water with the last shot of the day, a powerful slice into the well of an oasis. That evening we drove into a caravan and heard a strange story that was going round the bazaars of a new record for the course, though whether it was a record high or a record low, we couldn't make out.

Next morning I played our 12,174th stroke, exploding with my niblick from a camel's hoof print, and as the cloud of sand cleared away the Chief Caddy gave a great shout. We had reached the fairway. By way of celebration we issued a sniff of benzedrine all round and I wrote the White Hunter a post-dated cheque. Then we held our breath while Engelbrecht addressed the ball.

You've probably gathered by now that Engelbrecht over-swings. There's no doubt about that and I've often begged him to hold himself in check. Even so I was not prepared

for the deathly slice that followed. Leaving the clubhead at an angle of 45° the ball curved across the fairway in a vast drooping parabola.

The Chief Caddy put his head in his hands and rocked to and fro. 'Lord save us,' he moaned, 'plumb in the middle of the Butlin Holiday Camp.'

Caddies, bearers, psychiatrist, snake-charmer, and all gave vent to a deep groan.

Next to the Native Reserve the Butlin Holiday Camp is reckoned to be the fiercest Hazard of them all. The committee leased the site to Butlin after Salvador Dalí played his exhibition round on the course and complained that the last half was too easy. Since then many a surrealist golfer who's sliced into it has preferred to play his way quietly out to sea rather than face the prolonged stay which is often required.

It took us six weeks to play out of that Camp but my recollections are very vague because I went down with a severe go of sand-fly fever and was delirious all the time. I remember a fierce argument over the identity and ownership of the ball between the Chief Caddy and the Superintendent of the Children's Play Pen, and being chased between two endless beds of flaming geraniums by a 200-lb blonde in an American sailor's cap with *Kiss Me Quick* on it. I remember the camp chaplain trying to make Engelbrecht put five hundred pounds in the 'cuss box', and the torture of being got out of bed every other minute to play my stroke. The rest is a merciful blur, and I did not recover the priceless gift of consciousness which distinguishes us from the brutes until long after we had played our way out.

But our troubles were not yet over. The psychiatrist crocked up with a severe nervous breakdown and Engelbrecht's slice had to go untreated. There followed a succession of awkward lies from each of which I was too feeble to play out. Dr Edith Summerskill's Shopping Bag; Gandhi's Loin Cloth; Molotov's Desk in the Kremlin; the Lincoln Imp Tea Rooms; a *salon de décrottage* in old Marseilles; at each of them I foozled hopelessly and appealed to Engelbrecht: 'You got us into this, chum, and you got to get us out.' And little Engelbrecht grinned cheerfully back and swung his niblick. There was no daunting that indomitable dwarf.

It was eleven more months and ten more days after we had driven off the first tee and I had just played our 2,674,321,769th, a tricky little pitch out of the window of the 3.30 from Waterloo, when the Chief Caddy let out a yell and started dancing a reel. We had reached the green.

We took all Engelbrecht's wooden clubs away from him lest he should be tempted to press, because the green at Mooninghill is the size of an English county, and proceeded to foozle our way smoothly and quietly towards the huge hole. We should have done a lot better if the psychiatrist had been functioning to treat us for the anxiety neurosis which is one of the special features of that green. At last, after several hours of being too short, too far, and lipping the rim, we managed to tie up the ghostly hands that had been pushing our ball back from the hole and Engelbrecht sank a six-incher for 2,674,322,269.

The clubhouse was *en fête*. We could see its lights blazing from miles away in the inky night. And who should be the first persons we saw as we stumbled into the bar but Charlie

Wapentake and Nodder Fothergill. Not only were they not dead, but by a strange combination of circumstances, the legitimacy of which is still being debated hotly by the committee to this day, *they had done the hole in one.* It appears that before Charlie had a chance to play their second out of the Valley of Dry Bones, a huge vulture swooped down and flew off with the ball. Nodder and their White Hunter opened fire and winged the vulture who eventually dropped the ball down the vest of one of the competitors in a Japanese Women's Cross Country Race. She lost her way round the world while being chased by Harpo Marx and ran across the green and the ball slipped down the leg of her track shorts and rolled into the hole.

The celebrations lasted far into the century. My last recollection is of little Engelbrecht taking a header into the loving cup of flaming rum punch. 'Come on in,' he said, as he swam round and round, 'it's gloriously warm.'

# 4

# A THICK NIGHT AT THE PLANT THEATRE

*". . . the atmosphere was vibrating . . ."*

I SHALL ALWAYS remember the time – and a damned long time it was, too, as you'll realize in a minute – when Engelbrecht, the dwarf surrealist boxer, and I were slung out of the Old Plant Theatre of Varieties. It was during the first night of an arboreal epic entitled *Ash Before Oak*. We'd looked in there after dining with the Id and some of his chums at a new Black Market Restaurant that had opened next door to the Royal College of Surgeons' Museum.

The dinner was by way of celebrating the close season for Man-Hunting. Anyway, by the time we'd eaten our way through the menu of *recherché* Unmentionables, and drained the Ether decanter, I don't suppose there was a single one of us who was anywhere near in his right mind. So when Nodder Fothergill suggested dropping in at the Plant Theatre we, that is those of us who still retained the priceless gift of consciousness, were inclined to be enthusiastic. We bundled into the Id's huge black Fly and bowled off, whooping and shrieking like fiends.

We didn't realize just what we were in for. The fact is Plant Drama is apt to be a bit slow. All the parts are played by real plants, and plants, as you know, like to take their time about it. You can always rely on them for a sincere performance, but for a good deal of it you just have to sit there and watch them grow. It's a bit agonizing now and again, especially during love scenes. You'd scarcely credit the time it takes some of these diffident vegetables to make a pass at one another. Why, even a relatively fast worker like mistletoe, convolvulus, or bamboo, playing in a light Coward type comedy, can take three months over a proposal. As for the hardwood trees, well all I can tell you is that the curtain went up 5000 years ago on the famous New Forest Production of *King Lear* with an all-Oak cast and the audience are still there to this day.

Of course the Old Plant Theatre of Varieties isn't quite as slow as all that. They go in for Revue with choruses of cannas and herbaceous borders and orchids as stars, insects to carry the pollen about and an occasional bird to drop the seed from the OP side to the wings. But even so the tempo is a good deal slower than most people are used to.

The theatre itself is a cross between the Hollywood Bowl, Kew Gardens, and the old Leicester Square Empire. A good deal of it is in the open air, but the whole place is tangled up with gilt and greenery, plush and moss.

We arrived just before the curtain went up. The 'thing that was scarcely a thing' at the Almighty Whirlitzer was coming to the end of *Trees*, which is more or less the National Anthem, as you might say, of the plant world, and the atmosphere was vibrating with the intensity that invariably betokens a Plant's first night. Engelbrecht and I were sitting just in front of the Editor of *The Fly-Paper*, and I remember Engelbrecht saying sharply over his shoulder: 'If you don't stop buzzing, you God-damned blue-bottle, I shan't be able to hear the rustling of the leaves...'

That shows you he was a bit lit. Engelbrecht would never have spoken to an editor like that if he'd been stone cold sober. His sense of publicity is far too keen. Lizard Bayliss, who was sitting on his other side, was dreadfully upset. 'You didn't ought to have done that, kiddo,' he kept saying. 'You know how touchy he is. See! There goes one of his ruddy little correspondents buzzing off back to the office now. Now you mark my words, there'll be a nasty little bit of dirt about you spread all over his sticky front page tomorrow. Engelbrecht drunk again, I shouldn't wonder. Drunk again the night before a fight...And there'll be an inquiry and we shall lose the purse.' Just then the lights went out, the rain came down and the curtain went up on the first scene of: *Ash Before Oak.*

Now this, only we didn't know it at the time, represented a new venture on the part of a couple of old cowslips with more dew than sense who planned to strike a blow for the homely English Flora as opposed to all the exotic tropical blooms – orchids, frangipani, bougainvillæa, date palms, sandalwood – that had been monopolising the plant variety stage for so long. The star of the show, if you please, was a floppy hollyhock that the old cowslips had got a crush on at the last horticultural show. The whole thing was set in an English spring and summer – a wet one of course as you can tell by the title. The plot turned on a lot of cosy friendly rivalry between the Oak and the Ash as to which should be out first, with an idiotic garden party where the exotic tropical plants were made to look cheap and flashy beside the cottage garden brigade, attended by a ballet of cabbage whites.

The first scene was 'Somewhere In February'. The rain came down like a grey steel curtain, week after week, and nothing happened except a drip, drip, drip, plop, splash, plop. By the time it got round to March, and one or two green shoots were supposed to appear, most of us were beginning to get a bit restive. And when something went wrong with the wind machine so that it started blowing the March gale slap in our faces instead of back stage, we all turned as one man on Nodder Fothergill and asked what the hell he thought he was doing bringing us to our deaths of pneumonia in this hell hole. Nodder said how could he know it was going to be such a confounded flop, and we'd better turn it in and head for home.

But when we got up to go we had a nasty shock. Every exit was barred by oaks and ranged behind us was a dense row of whacking great thorn bushes, and when Charlie Wapentake protested, one of them bore down on him and lashed him to his seat with withies. Seems there's been a conspiracy on the part of the British Plant Council to make certain that British Plant actors and actresses should get a fair hearing.

Just then Engelbrecht gave me a nudge. 'Look over there,' he said. 'That's one consolation anyway.' I turned my head gingerly, expecting any moment to be pranged by a thorn, and was just in time to see the Editor of *The Fly-Paper* foiled in a phoney attempt to leave the theatre by way of the skylight. The thing that was 'barely a thing' shot him down with a blast on the Vox Humana, and he crash-dived into a spider's web.

Soon after that the star of the show, the floppy old hollyhock, made her first appearance as a young shoot. The Id blew a lecherous whistle but an oak boomed: 'No disrespect to British planthood, if you please?' And one of the thorn bushes gagged him with a bundle of brushwood.

That sobered us I can tell you. I mean to say you don't gag an elemental force like the Id as easily as all that. We sat dead silent till the end of the scene when they handed up a huge bouquet of raw meat to the hollyhock 'from her devoted admirers'.

Presently Lizard Bayliss began to whine that his feet were taking root in the floor. 'Can't you do nothing for me, kiddo?'

he whimpered. 'I'm turning into a ruddy shrub. I can feel it. If I don't get out of here soon I'll be all privet.'

Just then the scene changed again to the night of April 1st. A streaming wet night it was and black as your hat, so black you couldn't even see what the Ash and the Oak were supposed to be up to; the dialogue sounded to me like a lot of creaks. I was told afterwards the script called for glow-worms at this point, but the little devils had gone on strike; refused to shine while it was raining.

Engelbrecht whispered in my ear: 'Come on, chum. This is our chance! Let's try our luck back stage!' and the next thing I knew we were clambering through the branches of the Mighty Whirlitzer, heading for behind the scenes. We brushed past a lot of knobbly fungus that grew out of the oak and made it squeak, causing the Oak to muff one of his lines. He was a bit deaf that Oak; you could hear the prompter yelling at him like a foghorn: 'My tough breast gladdens at the touch of spring.' Then we dodged a bramble bush and a couple of pollarded willows that were larking about waiting for their cue – funny ideas of fun some of these trees have – and suddenly we found ourselves in a part of open country right up at the back of the stage. Engelbrecht paused to kick the heart out of a lettuce. 'The dressing rooms are over there,' he said, pointing vaguely into the murk.

I stumbled along in his wake, tripping over roots and shrubs and movable sods of turf waiting to come on in the next scene. I got the impression there was a good deal of discontent – more than is usual behind the scenes. The flowers were jealous of the trees and the trees were jealous of the shrubs. I heard a birch say she was damned if she would ever play a scene with a rhododendron in it again and in future she was going to have it stated plainly in her contract.

Next moment I tripped and fell flat on my face in a bed of pansies. Vicious little devils they were too; one of them bit me in the finger and they called me names I'd never even heard of. By the time I'd picked myself up Engelbrecht had disappeared.

That didn't worry me much. Engelbrecht, as you know, can generally be relied on to take care of himself. I wandered on until I came to a row of hot houses with blinds down over the glass and chinks of light showing through. These were the dressing rooms. Then from one of them with a huge great star painted on it, I heard a voice that sounded like Engelbrecht's yelling for help. I opened the door and peeped in.

There was Engelbrecht in the grips of a man-eating orchid; a wicked-looking brute it was: all kidney colour with great leprous looking blotches. It had got several tendrils round him and frankly I didn't think he stood a chance. 'Put me down at once,' Engelbrecht kept saying.

There wasn't much I could do; some other tropical growths were beginning to give me nasty looks and put out some suckers in my direction. But just then help came from

MANTRAP WITH PREY
After Henry Fuseli, RA, painted after an after-dinner story by Engelbrecht
*Original destroyed by gamma rays*

a totally unexpected quarter. A darned great beetle with a wingspread of two feet came whirring into the dressing room, and all the other plants began to grow towards it. They were waving their tendrils in a great state of agitation, and presently the man-eating orchid put Engelbrecht down, though it still kept a tendril round him, and bent its head closer to listen.

It appears this beetle was the agent for the orchids and while he was whirring about behind the scenes he'd managed to get a squint at the script and had realized that the whole thing was nothing but a plot to hold his clients up to ridicule, by loosing a good old English snowstorm on them in the middle of the flaming June ballet at the Garden Party. A pretty murderous wheeze, you must admit.

We held an indignation meeting on the spot. Some of the tropical growths were very keen on starting a forest fire, but Engelbrecht and I pointed out that with all that rain about it didn't stand a chance of catching, and it was too long to wait for the one-day heat wave that was due to coincide with the Hollyhock's Birthday Ball in the finale of the August act. Finally we persuaded them to let us organize some massed barracking behind the scenes during the May 1st twilight scene when the Oak was due to sing a baritone solo that went:

*Devonshire, Devonshire,*
*Sometimes I think it's Heavenshire,*
*Down there in Devonshire.*

We spread rumours right round the cast that the Oak hadn't been playing cricket and had been tapping the Ash's roots, which is the worst thing one tree can do to another – tantamount to arboreal murder. The Ash got to hear of it just as the Whirlitzer was starting up the bars of *Devonshire*, and the next moment the two forest giants were locked in mortal combat.

This was the signal for pandemonium. In only a few weeks the stage of the Plant Theatre was a solid mass of fighting, thrusting, scratching, pricking, sucking, draining, plants, flowers, shrubs, trees, mosses, ferns, and liverworts. In vain did the two cowslips, supporting between them a fainting Hollyhock, call out shrilly: 'Plants! Plants! Remember the traditions of the Profession! Remember your Contracts!' In vain did the thing that was 'barely a thing' pound out *Trees* at the Whirlitzer in an attempt to drown the terrible rustling, snapping and cracking, the screams of sundered roots and plucked stalks. And behind the scenes, egging them on with subtle botanical insults, was Engelbrecht...

It was not long before the Oak-Ushers and the Thorn Bush Chucker-Outs began joining in, and we were able to set about freeing the Id and the rest. A torrential downpour of rain, timed to coincide with the August Bank Holiday Flower Show Scene, was very useful in helping to loosen the soil. Even so we had to dig pretty deep to uproot Lizard Bayliss who had to put up with no end of chaff about his privet parts.

The last I saw of Engelbrecht he was staggering off back-stage again, bent nearly double under a shapeless bundle done up in cobweb from which could be heard a faint buzz. When I asked him what on earth he thought he was doing he told me he had a supper party date with a Giant Sundew.

# 5

# THE MAN-HUNT BALL

*". . . he pointed to a huge beehive-shaped parcel . . ."*

IT SEEMS to be generally agreed among surrealist sportsmen that the crownin' event of the season at which attendance is absolutely indispensable for Anything which is Anything, to say nothing of anybody who is anybody, is the famous millennial Man-Hunt Ball. It's a little as if you were to combine Lord's and Ascot, the Boat Race, the Finals of the Sudanese Belly Dancing Championships and the Ladies' Singles at Wimbledon, the Derby and the Peking Cockroach Racing Cup, and mix them up with the Waterloo Ball, the Caledonian Ball, and all the other sportin' championships, contests, celebrations, occasions and festivities under the sun…

And when I tell you that this was his very first Man-Hunt Ball, you will understand why Engelbrecht, the dwarf surrealist boxer, was in such a state of twitterin' excitement, so unlike his usual deadpan sangfroid, when I met him and his manager Lizard Bayliss underneath the Station Clock to travel down together to Nightmare Abbey for old Iddesleigh's house-party.

'I don't know what's come over you, kiddo,' Lizard was saying. 'Keep still, can't you. Why, you're as excited as a…'

'…As a young surrealist sportsman before his first Man-Hunt Ball,' piped little Charlie Wapentake who joined us at that moment. 'I say, what the dev have you got there?' He pointed to a huge beehive-shaped parcel at which Engelbrecht kept glancin' coyly.

'That's his fancy dress, that is,' said Lizard sadly.

Then, after a little more chat and showers of chaff, we all moved off to platform N where the underground special for Nightmare Abbey, locally known as The Town Drain, was drawn up waitin', already packed tight with surrealist sportsmen, and their fair partners with them, these last includin' a bevy of ravishin' mechanical contrivances, some of them so fetchin' in their discreet travellin' clothes of brown paper and string that Chippy de Zoëte whispered in my ear that he hardly knew how to keep his pliers off them.

Indeed, what with one Thing and Another, and the ten-gallon flask of Embalmers Fluid which generous old

Lizard would insist on passin' round, we scarcely noticed the nights fly past or felt the shock when we cannoned into the tremblin' old buffers at Nightmare Abbey Halt.

Nightmare Abbey was packed out. I found I'd been allotted a poky little oubliette in the tower at the end of the Bachelor's Wing. When I started beefin' about it old Lamia Lobb, the Id's housekeeper, said I was lucky not to be sharin' a coffin in the crypt like Nodder Fothergill and Chippy de Zoëte. She was an ex-witch whom the Id had winged out Witch-Shooting and brought home and tamed. Lizard and Engelbrecht were just underneath me and I could hear their conversation through a hole in their ceiling. 'I don't know how you think you're going to get them to stay on at all, kiddo, much less to stay on in formation,' Lizard was saying. Engelbrecht didn't sound quite as perky as usual but I couldn't catch what he said because it was drowned in a sudden blast of hummin'. I surmised the plucky little chap was trying to cover up his nervousness. Even I, old hand that I am, was feelin' the strain. My hands were shakin' so I could scarcely do up the straps of my Surrealist Huntsman's strait-waistcoat.

THE Man-Hunt breakfast is scheduled for an hour before midnight and I always like to be down early for it. It didn't take me long to slip on my trusty old pillar-box over my strait-waistcoat. Then I scuttled down the corkscrew staircase past Engelbrecht's door. The hummin' was louder than ever and Lizard Bayliss was giving tongue with a series of intermittent yells that sounded as if he was being pricked all over.

The Great Hall was beginnin' to fill up with surrealist sportsmen of all shapes and sizes. I joined Nodder Fothergill and Charlie Wapentake over by the fireplace for an eyeopener of Vampire's Blood, and we stood there coughin' and chokin' and slappin' each other on the back, discussin' famous runs of the past and criticizin' the dresses. You see, as Master of the Man-Hunt, the Id always insists that the Hunt which precedes the Ball shall provide the run of the season. If anything goes wrong Bones Barlow the huntsman and Rollo Chatteridge the Whip get the lashin' of their lives. It's up to them to see that the Kill takes place in the Ballroom so that the Ball can begin right away.

Presently there was a tremendous blast on the huge Man-Huntsman's Horn and we took our places for the ceremonial entry of the Master. I was beginning to think that Engelbrecht had missed the bus. Then I heard the hummin' again, only louder still, and I saw hurryin' into the hall, Lizard Bayliss, his face swollen to four times the natural size and covered in blue bag. Behind him was Engelbrecht. He was dressed in nothing but a swarm of bees. They had assumed the formation of a faultlessly cut ridin' coat and breeches. Next moment the Id was in his place, raisin' his skull for the first toast and the Man-Hunt breakfast had begun.

Soon there was another blast on the Horn and the two Ghoulies staggered in with a covered-in cage containin' the Quarry. These Ghoulies are something like the Devon and Somerset stag-hunt's tufters, but in addition to markin' down the Quarry they have to bag it and bring it back.

There had been rumours that the Quarry this time was something quite exceptional, and when the Id got on his feet he was beamin' all over. 'Gentlemen of the Man-Hunt,' he roared, 'it gives me much pleasure to introduce to you our Quarry who will, I feel sure, mark an occasion in the annals of the Man-Hunt. We've hunted all sorts of types in the past. Schoolmasters, Stockbrokers, Bishops, Generals, and now and then, but only when scent was very poor, a Dartmoor Convict or two. But this, gentlemen, is the first time we have ever had for our Quarry' – here he stepped up to the cage and twitched aside the cover: 'a carted prime minister.' You should have heard the roar that went up.

Then the Id's family chaplain, old Father Carfax (unfrocked from all the eastern churches in turn for Wizardry) read the burial service and the pack, huge great coal-black brutes of the true Baskerville breed, big as bulls, bounded into the hall and began sniffin' at the cage and bayin' like the devil. The Quarry was sprayed with 'My Sin', just in case his natural scent shouldn't be strong enough, and dosed with a special fiery concoction of Bones Barlow's, guaranteed to make him 'lep like a hippogriff'. Not, as Charlie Wapentake pointed out, that there was really any need for it in this case, as most prime ministers are in such a state of terror these days that they'll lep like hippogriffs anyway. Then hounds were whipped off and the Ghoulies staggered away with the cage to Hangman's Copse, traditional covert for 'Releasing the Quarry', and we all trooped off to the stables, mounted our surrealist steeds and jogged off to the meet.

There's no hard and fast rule about mounts out Man-Huntin' and in addition to the ordinary run of equine beasts – horses, zebras, unicorns, and so on, you get a pretty fair selection of curiosities all accordin' to what sort of a line – moorland, jungle, desert or big city – their riders think the Quarry is going to take. The Id, with about three hundred yards of Man-Huntsman's horn slung round him, was sitting a deuced great hippogriff which threatened to become airborne any moment. I couldn't see Engelbrecht at first. Then, just as I was draining my stirrup, Chippy de Zoëte tapped me on the knee with his crop. (I was going to see a good deal of Chippy at that hunt because we were both ridin' centaurs and they liked to stick close together and talk philosophy out of the corner of their mouths.) 'Look up there,' Chippy said, 'there's pluck for you!'

I looked up and saw Engelbrecht, perched way up on the worst Nightmare in the Id's stables. Even the Id was scared of her. Lizard Bayliss was clinging to the stirrup. 'Have you ever ridden before, kiddo?' he was sayin'. 'Well promise me you never will again.'

JUST then the Id roared 'Hounds, Gentlemen, please!' and the field moved off at a trot towards Hangman's Copse – all that is except the lady president of the RSPCA who couldn't get her rocking-horse to start and the Fakir of Benares who was having trouble with the girths of his special Bed O'Nails saddle.

The hunt started off much as usual. Rollo and Bones put hounds in to draw the covert from the Warlock Edge end downhill towards Witches' Wen and the River Alph. The rest of us hung about outside the covert tryin' to decide which was the least odious of the ways through it in the event of the PM breakin' at the far side. Not a hound had spoken yet but they were forcin' their way into that fearful, fiend-infested undergrowth, with growin' excitement. We heard a yelp followed by a cry of 'Baskerville has it.' Then the Id's voice roaring 'Hark! Hark!' and Bones Barlow's renowned and blood-curdling screech of 'Gone Away.' Then babel broke out as hounds convergin' from every quarter, flung themselves howlin' on the line.

I must say that PM put on a turn of speed which was quite surprisin' in a Quarry of such a sedentary occupation. By the light of the phosphorescent slaver from Baskerville's muzzle I caught a glimpse of little legs in their striped trousers flashin' like propeller blades. Then he made a terrific spurt and drew away into the darkness.

Chippy and I did our best to go with Engelbrecht and give him a lead, but it wasn't easy because that damned Nightmare of his was simply all over the place. Hounds ran devilish fast after breakin' covert. There was a thick fog. Perfect for scent. Not a check for days. We galloped over moorland and meadow, flew banks and fences, crashed through gorse thickets. Then gradually the country changed to town. 'Unsportin' little beast,' said Chippy de Zoëte, as our centaurs changed feet on top of an Odeon and plunged down into an allotment, 'he's makin' a bee-line for home.'

As dawn broke we were checked in Parliament Square. The Quarry had gone to ground.

Bones Barlow and Rollo Chatteridge were puttin' the terriers down a manhole. Engelbrecht, I noticed, was havin' a spot of bother with his huntin' kit. Those bees were showin' a distressin' tendency to break formation. Suddenly with a yell of 'God damn it, there go my breeches!' he dug his heels into his Nightmare and galloped off in pursuit of the nether half of the swarm. 'Pity,' said Chippy de Zoëte, 'I'd hoped he might get the brush.'

BY means of some absolutely consummate huntsmanship – and a good deal of dynamite – Bones Barlow succeeded in boltin' the PM from the cellar of the House of Commons. Rollo Chatteridge with three couple of Baskervilles headed him off from the continental boat train and the Id laid the rest of the pack on the line and hunted him along the Great West Road. He gave us the slip near Northolt and became airborne. We clung on to the scent but we had to hunt him across three continents before we finally turned him back to the Nightmare Country, and 'killed' in the ballroom.

The Man-Hunt Ball was at its height. Charlie Wapentake and various members of the house party were gallantly toastin' Lamia Lobb in her own surgical boot filled with

formalin. The fiddlers were strikin' up the homicidal strains of *D'ye ken Jack Ketch?* and surrealist sportsmen were gallopin' in the arms of Ghosts, Gorgons, and even a few Girls, when a naked dwarf dismounted from a limping Nightmare and knocked at the gate of Nightmare Abbey. He was accompanied by an object that looked like a man but whose features and limbs were indistinguishable on account of the presence all over them of a swarm of bees…

We led Engelbrecht into the cloakroom and persuaded the bees to change over. This time they assumed the formation of faultless evenin' dress. The man was revealed as an American president.

'Well, kiddo,' said Lizard Bayliss, checkin' himself just in time from clappin' Engelbrecht on the back, 'you certainly got your man.'

One school of thought wanted to give Engelbrecht both brushes, masks and all eight pads, but, as Nodder Fothergill, who is hon sec of the Man-Hunt and more or less the authority on minor matters of ritual, pointed out, you've got to observe some rules even in Man-Huntin'. However, the Id was so delighted with Engelbrecht's pluck and persistence that he insisted on makin' him a fully-fledged member of the Man-Hunt on the spot, and while I stuck on the Death's Head Buttons, Lizard Bayliss got a bottle of red ink and started dyein' the bees pink.

# 6

# THE ONE THAT NEARLY GOT AWAY

*". . . Hook me in the hump . . ."*

OF ALL the events in the Surrealist Sporting Calendar few attract such a passionately excited following as the Annual Angling Championship, held in the Canal round behind the Gasworks, just where the Town Drain comes in.

Unlike the ordinary humdrum disciple of Izaak Walton, your Surrealist Piscator can always be certain of catching something – generally something damned dangerous, if you ask me – and many's the deathly struggle I've witnessed on the bank as terrified Anglers tried to put back Things that would have been far better never hooked. It was, therefore, with the keenest anticipation, and no little misgiving, that I accepted the invitation of my friend Engelbrecht, the dwarf surrealist boxer, an all-round sportsman if ever there was one, to make up a party to watch him compete for the trophy.

A room had been booked for me at The Fisherman's Eternal Rest, and when I arrived I found the little bar-parlour thronged with old friends and fiends, all keen amateurs of the gentle art, fortifying their nerves with rounds of double mandragora laced with poppy against the morrow's encounters with the perils of the deep. Meanwhile, in the Hashish room at the end of the passage, Dr Sadismus, the surrealist surgeon, then at the height of his fame owing to his daring operation for the removal of a human finger from the bowels of a sewing machine, was organising, with the assistance of a posse of psychiatrists, a First Aid Post.

The talk was all of the Catch that might be expected. In accordance with his usual general custom, the Id, that munificent patron of Surrealist Sport, had contributed lavishly to stocking the Canal, and some really sensational captures were anticipated. Rumour had it that the Prize was a 600-year-old giant pike from the Fens, the same who in 1448 snatched the Bishop of Ely from his mule as he rode the towpath.

'You stand a fine chance of hooking him, my wee man, chaffed Chippy de Zoëte, patting Engelbrecht on the head. 'Dwarfs are his favourite bait.'

Just then Lizard Bayliss, my friend's devoted but highly strung manager, who had been for a stroll along the canal bank, tottered in and collapsed in a trembling heap. 'There's Things in that there water that never ought to have been thought of,' he told us.

After a restless night disturbed more than once by screams, I hurried down to find the rest of our party with grave faces. News had just been brought that the lock-keeper and his entire family had been dragged under.

The beat Engelbrecht had drawn for the early morning rise was a stretch of jet black water between the Jubilee Gasometer and the Municipal Slaughter House. A dank mist lay over the canal. The vampire bats were out in swarms. The bot-fly waltzed in virid clouds. You could hardly have had a better surrealist fishing day. From their stand on top of the gasometer the Band of the Asylum Workers Union struck up the *March of*

REPULSE BOARDERS!

After Hieronymus Bosch

*The original canvas hangs on the north wall of the Piscator's, or Liar's, Room at the Surrealist Sportsman's Club*

*the Wooden Zombies*. Presently the quavering tones of Dreamy Dan, the surrealist umpire, announced the start of play.

'Crikey,' said Lizard Bayliss, 'do you see what I see?'

Floating on the surface of the water was a fleet of five pound notes. Lizard was in the act of bending down to pick one up when a voice behind him said: 'I shouldn't touch that if I were you. It's surface bait laid on from below to catch the unwary fisherman.'

It was our old friend the Oldest Member who had tottered out of his tomb swathed in a shroud of Donegal tweed to see how we were faring. Under his supervision we assembled Engelbrecht's tackle, a somewhat eclectic assortment that included a rod as big as a crane and a float with a great chapel bell attached. Then Lizard Bayliss backed the Black Maria containing the bait down to the water's edge.

There was some heated discussion over the choice of bait. Engelbrecht wanted to fish a Barnet By-Pass, a beautifully made facsimile of a suburban housewife with a lot of brightly coloured feathers in her hat, just the kind of gaudy affair calculated to catch the eye of the tyro. But the OM counselled a more sober-looking lure known as a College Chaplain, one of Clarkson's most skilful pieces of human dry-fly-tying, in cork and composition with bespoke tailoring and a neat little hump to conceal the hook. 'Did you ever see anything so lifelike?' he said.

'Too damned lifelike altogether,' said Lizard. 'Lumme, did you see that? I believe he winked at me.'

'I hope he did no such thing,' said the OM severely. 'Fishing with human bait is barred. We had to disqualify de Lautréamont for that in '53.'

Our preparations were now complete. Engelbrecht took a firm grip on the rod and brought all his dwarf strength to bear. The first cast pulled down the façade of a stationer's shop in Fore Street. The second hooked a tray of glass eyes. The third was a fizzer. Fathom after fathom of line shot out and away out of sight into the mist. But when we took roll call afterwards Lizard Bayliss was missing.

Presently there was an earsplitting peal from the chapel bell far out across the black water. Engelbrecht began reeling in. Soon we caught sight of a vast domed shape looming through the mist. It was the float with Lizard Bayliss sitting on top of it. We gaffed him ashore. It was obvious he would never be fit to fish again so we packed him off to the psychiatrist's.

By now the canal bank was a scene of frightful carnage but precious little piscage. Nodder Fothergill, on our right, had landed something I never expected to see outside the canvases of Hieronymus Bosch and was fighting a losing battle trying to put it back. Bones Barlow had plunged in after a Nereid and had his waders rotted off by acid. Little

Charlie Wapentake had fouled the Grendel family *mère et fils*. So critical, indeed, did the situation become that just before lunch the order was given to Repel Boarders. We all dropped our rods and rushed to the rescue of whoever needed help most.

The score at lunch time was depressing. Several of our best anglers had either been dragged under, pulled out to sea, or else were raving in the schizophrenic ward. Father Carfax, the Id's Chaplain, had been lost with all hands during a plucky exorcism ceremony. Some interesting inanimate objects had been caught, including a calculating machine which, as the OM observed, would come in handy for telling fishing stories. Salvador Dalí had landed a chest of drawers of fifty-seven pounds weight, the contents of which had to be sent to the local police. But no one had had a bite from the man-eating pike and there was a rumour that Chippy de Zoëte had been seen slipping some sticks of dynamite into his waistcoat pocket.

After lunch we drew the Fever Hospital Bend, a ticklish stretch where you have to fish off a narrow asphalt track with a fifty foot drop into the Rubbish Dump at your back. I attached a lure known as The Hanged Man and we cast far out into the murk, now thickened by fumes from the chemical works. 'They can never resist this one,' said Engelbrecht with typical angler's optimism. But they could. When the bell tolled and we reeled in we found nothing save a shipwrecked pleasure party clinging to the float. The bait was untouched except for a notice which some under-water character had tied round its neck. It read: '*Insufficiently Verisimilitudinous. Better Luck Next Time.*'

We showed it to the Oldest Member who was engrossed in Chetham's *Vade Mecum*. 'That's the Fisher King,' he said. 'A mythological figure who haunts these waters. Reputed to be a cousin of the Id's. Got a very keen sense of humour. He collected one of those new pens that write underwater from one of our members last year.'

A rattle of musketry on our left denoted that yet another landing party had been repulsed. But still not a bite.

The Oldest Member looked up from Sir Humphrey Davey's *Salmonia* which he had been perusing. 'I'm afraid you're having very poor sport,' he said. 'The catch of the day so far is a Seven League Boot.'

Engelbrecht was down at the reel end of the rod. He rang through on the 'phone to ask me to come and take a turn, while he had a chat with the OM. When he came back his face was set and grim. He was wearing a Frogman's suit of black india rubber and a clerical collar. 'Hook me, pal,' he said, 'hook me in the hump.'

'But dwarfie,' I said, 'you're not going in yourself?'

'It's the only way,' he said.

'But you're human, aren't you? You'll be disqualified.'

'The OM says not. He says it's all right if you bait your own hook. You'll hold the rod for me, pal?'

'Well,' I said. 'I hope you know what you're doing.'

'I hope I do too,' he said.

'Greater love hath no angler than this,' said the voice of the OM behind us.

I fixed the hook tight into the artificial hump and paid out enough line to reach all the way. I gave the hook a final tug to make sure it was good and firm. Then I cast. The dwarf-baited hook flew out through the thick night air far over the water. It fell with a light splash. I reeled in a few hundred fathoms to keep him riding on top of the water and gave the line a couple of jerks to make it seem as if he was drowning. Then I lit my pipe.

Presently I heard Engelbrecht's voice on the intercom. 'They're coming for me, pal,' he said. 'I can see their eyes all round me. It's just a question which one gets me first. Soon as you hear me holler you got to strike for all you're worth.'

Next moment the bell pealed out the Angelus and Engelbrecht's voice yelled in my ear: 'Strike like beggary.' I turned on the donkey engine full steam ahead and struck.

The line ran out at a rate of knots. There was silence for some time. Then Engelbrecht came through again. 'You there, pal? He's hooked good. It's the giant pike all right.'

'How do you know?'

'He's swallowed me and I just picked up a Bishop's mitre with the name Ely on the sweat band. Play him, pal. Play him for all you're worth. You got to land him before the season ends.'

In the months that followed I played that pike all over the network of our inland waterways, in and out of drains and culverts and subterranean streams known only to spæleologists. Sometimes when the line was right out I had to take the train to keep up with him. And always the Oldest Member was at my elbow ready to give sage counsel. 'Whatever happens we must head him off from the Fens,' he kept telling me. 'Black Fen, which is his home water, is known to be bottomless.'

It was the last week of the season and Engelbrecht had just phoned through, very faint, to say that his rations had run out. We were streaking along the Manchester Ship Canal with mighty few fathoms in hand. 'I'm afraid we've lost him,' said the Oldest Member. 'You'll have to order your little pal to abandon fish.' With a sob in my voice I told Engelbrecht to unhook himself. Suddenly we rounded a bend and caught sight of a bunch of Theological Students out for a walk with the Bishop at their head. The pike must have seen them too. He leapt in a great green-yellow arc for the bank. But he was too weak, and before his jaws could close, the Bishop, an old sportsman if ever there was one, had gaffed him in the gills with his umbrella. The ordination candidates formed a chain, clasping each other by the waist.

After a tremendous struggle we got him ashore and wired for Doctor Sadismus, who removed Engelbrecht, little the worse for wear. There was a good deal of controversy in surrealist piscatorial circles, but it was finally decided that the Catch should stand. And you can see the pike stuffed, with the Bishop of Ely's mitre underneath, in the Fisherman's Eternal Rest.

# 7

# ENGELBRECHT AND THE DEMON BOWLER

*". . . muttering to himself and sucking his fingers . . ."*

THE NEWS that I, *AN Other*, had been selected, as twelfth man, to support the eleven which was to play the MCC's Touring Side at the Nightmare Abbey Cricket Week was brought to me, late, as I lay in the great, grey, brain-shaped Dream-Room of the Surrealist Sportsman's Club. I had just time to pack my vampire-bat and catch the Town Drain.

When I alighted from my fly, Platform 666 at the Ultimate Terminus, that night, was a sight to make sore eyes sorer. Over its limitless expanses swarmed cricketers of all shapes and sizes, clothed in white samite, mystic, wonderful. The atmosphere was vibrant with keenness. Giants, Dwarfs, Fragments, Freaks of all kinds, played forward strokes from improvised wickets – lamp-posts, newspaper-kiosks, porters' legs. Presently, amid the throng, I discerned my old friend Engelbrecht, the dwarf surrealist boxer, in the act of late cutting a neon bulb that swung in from the off, delivered right round the station clock by the cunning hand of Chippy de

Zoëte. Lizard Bayliss, my diminutive friend's pessimistic manager, was keeping wicket behind a Stonehenge-like structure of luggage and station architecture. He was muttering to himself and sucking his fingers which had been damaged by some of the improvised 'leathers' with which he was being pelted and which ranged from grape-fruit and Witch Balls to Tommy Prenderghast's pet hedgehog, Chattox, and the Globe at Swanage.

The Terminus Bell tolled and we all surged forward as one flannelled fool, singing the Long Stop's Chorus from Sir Henry Newbolt's Opera *Middle and Leg*, towards Platform N, where the Town Drain was gaping at the seams to receive us. I bought the latest best-seller, *How to Win Over Fiends and Influence Paranoiacs*, from a strolling stall and settled down in my padded corner.

When I recovered the priceless gift of consciousness which distinguishes us from the brutes, I was lying on my back in a clearing surrounded by clumps of Old Man's Beard. Amnesia, that all too frequent occupational complaint of the surrealist sportsman, had me in its grip. 'Where am I?' I asked.

'In the deep,' said Lizard Bayliss, who was bending over me, fanning me with a dock leaf. 'You've stopped one on the conk from W G Grace. We was sent out here, you and me and the dwarf and some more, at the beginning of the last over, as part of Prenderghast's leg-trap. "Send all those ruddy duffers right out into the deep," Prendy roars. So we marches off here and here we've been ever since. We've beaten off several attacks from Fuzzy Wuzzy. The Gatling's jammed and the Colonel's dead and we're still waiting for the voice of a schoolboy to rally the ranks. The Dwarf caught the leather and he's trying to break through with it to Square Leg. You better lie still. You been acting queer for days.'

Just then a message came through on the Bush Telegraph to say it was Over. We struck Camp and began the long trek to the other end of the field.

The appearance of our sadly depleted party in the neighbourhood of the Pitch was the signal for a burst of clapping. Engelbrecht, it seemed, had got through without dropping the catch. The Men in White were now in the act of overpowering Dr Grace. They disarmed him of his bat and hauled him, still struggling, from the wicket.

But the scoreboard, at 903 for 1, gave us little encouragement, and the black flag on the abbey tower drooped at half-mast. At the Pavilion End, our skipper, the Id, was deep in conference with his lieutenants. As we hacked our way through the palisades of cow parsley and cronesbane that flanked the outfield, we looked back for the last time. The Id had tossed the ball to the Village Idiot.

Victor Trumper came striding out of the pavilion and took middle and leg.

Presently a rumour began to reach us out in the deep that the Village Idiot had found a spot. It appears that several generations of his forebears had been buried in Murderers' Meadow before it was enclosed and turned into a cricket field. The thunder of Dr Grace's hooves had considerably disturbed their rest and now the VI, by some primitive, atavistic, homing instinct, had found his spot right on the crown of his great-great-grandfather's skull which was anchored a few feet outside the off stump. The result was some absolutely unplayable stuff.

With his first ball he sent a joyful death rattle through Trumper's wicket. His second caught Ranjit Singhi between wind and water. By the end of the over the score was 1001 for 5. But during the luncheon interval Dr Grace and a couple of JPs, of which the visiting team had no shortage, pulled a fast one on us, by having him certified. The rest of our bowling was poor stuff and though Salvador Dalí's lobs soared up to dizzy heights and came down accompanied by unmentionable objects, they took no wickets.

The monster innings dragged on. Summer was past and gone and with the decay of the vegetation we in the outfield were exposed not only to the elements but also to the scrutiny of our skipper. I was compelled to suspend my monograph on *Varieties of the Cuckoo-Spit* while Lizard Bayliss had to fold up the Crown and Anchor Board with which he had been trimming the cricket correspondents of *The Fly-Paper*. Soon afterwards, however, Dr Grace appealed against floods and snow and we retired to winter quarters.

The recess was spent in feverish planning and our side's Headquarters in the Refractory Wing of the *Three Jolly Cricketers* was like an SS Sabotage College. But against such an experienced tactician as Dr Grace our best-laid schemes miscarried. Play had scarcely been resumed under a tropical sun when the mine which Chippy de Zoëte's Sappers had dug under the leg stump was detected and rendered harmless. One after another, explosive bats, winged bails, and gyroscopically controlled balls were detected and appealed against while the plucky decisions of our staunch umpire were set at naught by the MCC. In the end it was only fear of utter exhaustion and

premature death which caused the visitors to declare their innings closed at 3,333,333 for 9; truly, as the Editor of *The Fly-Paper* remarked in his leading article, a formidable total.

If our batting was on a par with our bowling – and despite Salvador Dalí's boast that he would carry his chest-of-drawers right through the innings, there was no reason to suppose it would be any different – we were all set for an innings defeat. It was generally agreed that the side needed stiffening, though some defeatists were even beginning to mutter that the sooner it was over the better, that cricket with its rigid code and static tempo was not our game.

The morning our innings opened, I was leaning over the pavilion rails, watching the groundsmen stoke up the furnace in which the MCC kept their Demon Bowler between overs, when Chippy de Zoëte, our vice-captain, tapped me on the shoulder. 'I'm awfully sorry, Other, old boy,' he said, 'but I'm going to ask you to stand down. It's for the good of the side, of course. Fact is we want to play Another in your place.'

I said: 'Of course.' I couldn't very well say anything else. After all, the family motto of the Others is 'They also serve.' And by George when I heard who my substitute was, I let out a great cheer. For it was none other than the Willow King himself, the British Wood-Demon, the tutelary deity of the Game. It seems he had fallen into a decline a long time gone because of the deathly stillness which had crept into the sacred ritual, and being subject, like all Willows, to melancholia, he had got himself into a very bad way indeed. In fact when the Id's talent spotters finally ran him to earth he was in the Weeping Willow Ward of an Asylum for Trees. However, they strapped pads over his roots and tied his Free Foresters' scarf round his trunk, and he perked up no end; by the time they reached the ground he was playing strokes all round the wicket so lightning fast it looked as if every one of his branches was a bat. All we needed was someone to stay in with him and stonewall while he scored.

The innings opened like a dream. The Id decided to waste no time and sent in the Willow King with the Marquis de Sade to keep him company. We had expected WG might appeal, but when he saw the God of Cricket in person he doffed his cap in homage, unwound his MCC scarf, 'the oriflamme of English Cricket', as CB Fry once called it, and hung it from a convenient branch. When the applause had subsided the WK took guard. The umpire shouted play. The door of the asbestos oven swung open and with a puff of smoke and a blast of flame the Demon Bowler roared out on his scorching run.

The ease with which that old tree opened his shoulders and drove the first five balls out of the ground and tapped the sixth towards cover point for a single became positively monotonous, especially when he had repeated the process for a few hundred overs.

The score stood at 333,333 for 0 when disaster overtook us. De Sade tripped over a sylph at midwicket and was stumped before he could get back to his crease. In the next over the Demon Bowler took 6 wickets for no runs. Clearly, one more mishap like this would be our undoing. It was not long in coming. Salvador Dalí was the next man in, but when at the end of another triumphant over the Willow King snicked his single, it was found that he had taken root in the ground and could not leave his crease. '*Atras*!' he shouted gallantly in Spanish, and waved Dalí back to his crease. The first ball of the Demon Bowler's next over splintered the Catalan sportsman's chest of drawers as if it had been matchwood. We afterwards discovered it was matchwood.

333,363 for 7 and the DB had five balls in which to take three wickets. He went through Chippy de Zoëte, put in late to stiffen the tail, and Charlie Wapentake, like an eel through milk.

333,363 for 9; all the hours on the clock to play and the last man in. Reeling from the smite of his dynamic captain's hand on his shoulder, the dwarf Engelbrecht stumbled out of the pavilion and made his way towards his wicket, which towered above him like the pillars of some vast monument. Testily he took guard and settled into his crease like a flea in a crack.

Wham! The DB sent down a perfect length express dead on the middle stump. Casting himself into the air like a soul waltzing in hell, the dwarf just managed to reach it with the tip of his bat, and deflect it over the wicket-keeper's head. By way of celebration the WK burst into bud.

Three more balls to go. The sun was blazing down, but the Willow King stretched out his leaves to make shade for the valiant dwarf. Again the Demon Bowler let fly with all the vice of his sinewy black arm. And once again the dwarf deflected the spheroid.

After that it was plain sailing. Myth and Dwarf were all set for the finest last wicket stand in the history of the game. Seasons flew by. Our total had reached an astronomical figure, and the Id was trying to summon up courage enough to declare, when a very old man with a scythe and an hour-glass came wandering towards the pitch.

'I've come to put a stop to all this,' he said in a creaking, leathery voice. Lifting his scythe for a back stroke he glided forward towards the pitch. There was a flutter and a scurry from the MCC. Then we saw that WG had gone down on his knees in front of the Willow King, edging right up close to his trunk. The Willow King put down a leafy branch and next moment there was nothing to be seen except the tree, and twenty-two yards away the Dwarf Engelbrecht chasing a cabbage white.

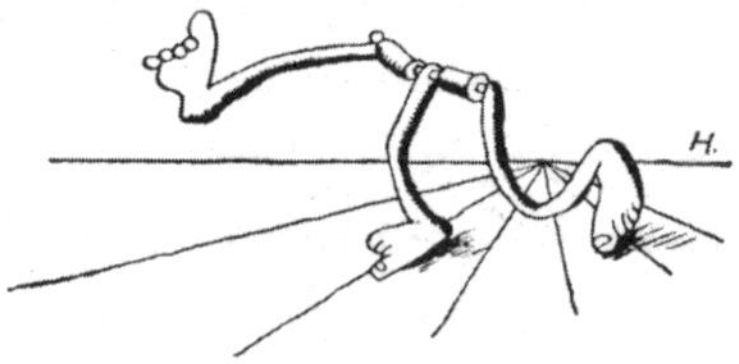

# 8

# THE DAY WE PLAYED MARS

*". . . our frail human forwards are too light . . ."*

THIS IS the story of how Engelbrecht, the dwarf surrealist boxer, wins his Global Football Cap. It's a story the oldest members still whisper in the Ghost Room of the Surrealist Sportsman's Club, a story of indomitable courage, and no little cunning, winning through against overwhelming odds.

Engelbrecht has never played surrealist football before and his delight at finding his name, just above *Engels, F,* in the list – a sizeable work in many volumes – of the team to play Mars in the Final of the Interplanetary Challenge Cup, leads to a celebration in which we all take part.

The Final of the Interplanetaries is played off on the Moon, and months before the kick-off all sorts of vehicles – everything from ordinary space-ships to beams, dreams, mediums, and telepathic wave-patterns – start arriving with the players. There's a pause for rest and reorientation; then they begin trooping into the vast Metamorphosis or Changing Room. Engelbrecht and I blow in in a rocket with the usual party of our Skipper's intimates. We've been training strictly on hashish and mescaline, and by the time we arrive on the Ground it's a job to sort us out from our hallucinations.

The Lunar Twickenham is a boundless plain of glassy black lava pitted with craters. The Larger Ball is considered *de rigueur*. It has to be something pretty sizeable to keep in play at all, though, as Charlie Wapentake says, it's a bit nightmarish trying to dribble with a thing like a Roc's egg.

Dreamy Dan, our old-time surrealist umpire, is thought to be too biased, as well as a trifle slow for such a commando-type operation. The new referee is Cecil B de Mille, picked for his crowd work. Presently he sends a message to ask the Id to scrabble along and meet the Martian Skipper in a neutral crater for final briefing. So off the Old Master trots, accompanied by Chippy de Zoëte, his Vice. When they come back they're shaking all over and Chippy de Zoëte's chest-wig, which he had made at Clarkson's to strike terror into the opposing forwards, has turned white as fleece. From which we deduce that this year's Martian team includes some pretty formidable Entities. So tough, indeed, does the opposition appear that it's decided to try a very unorthodox ploy and put the full side, the entire human race, into the field straight away.

The opening ceremony is held as usual. There's a silent tribute to the honour of William Webb Ellis, that Glorious Precursor of Surrealist Sport, the Rugby Schoolboy who first ran with the Ball. Then the Band strikes up the *Supersonic Symphony* – a rather unfortunate choice for it brings half the Grandstand down with a crash. After which we take the Field.

Even I, old hand as I am, haven't quite bargained for the procession of Giant Monstrosities that come filing out of the Visitors Entrance. When Lizard Bayliss, Engelbrecht's pessimistic manager, catches sight of them he tries to beat it back to the Changing Room, but the crush of characters is too thick.

MARTIAN FORWARD LINE
Painted on the spot by Official Surrealist Sports Artist, John (Mad) Martin
*Original in the Id's Gallery of Surrealist Sporting Pictures*

It's our kick-off. It takes a bit of doing to sort us all out, but by the next full moon de Mille has us well in hand. I've been given a cosy little assignment, narking to the Central Captain's Committee on the Wing Forwards, so I take Engelbrecht under my wing and pilot him.

The whistle blows and Melchisedek takes the kick. Nebuchadnezzar follows up and gathers it. He passes to Nero, Nero to Attila, Attila to the Venerable Bede, the Venerable Bede to Ethelred the Unready, who knocks on into a crater. De Mille screams for a scrum. Engelbrecht tries to climb down into the thick of it. 'You keep out of that,' I tell him. 'The idea! A dwarf trying to scrum down between Henry VIII and Cetewayo. You'd get pulped.'

De Mille rolls the ball down an inclined plane right into the centre of the great heaving mass. Anak and Harold Hardrada, our hookers, get their toes round it. But our frail human forwards are too light for those great Martian thugs. We can't possibly hold them. Our only hope is to heel out quickly before they can crush us against the sides of the crater. It doesn't take Charlie Marx, our scrum-half long to twig this, and as we peer down over the lip we can hear his harsh bark of 'Heel! You *teufels*! Heel in the name of History!' And heel they do, but only just in time. As Charlie Marx gathers the ovoid from Bismarck's boot, our front line breaks and the Martian phalanx comes crashing through. Marx slings it back to Fred Engels, his fly-half. Then he's down in a sea of boots and backsides. 'You've got to hand it to old Charlie,' says Tommy Prenderghast, 'he may be nasty tempered but he's the nippiest scrum-half in this world or the next. Well, we'd better be heading for Goal. Can I give you chums a lift?'

But Fred Engels has seen it coming and had time to get his life-line organized. He passes it up to Gladstone who makes a present of it to Blondin. And before you can say 'I told you so', Blondin's away out on his tight-rope with the Giant Ball at his feet. It's a great moment, one of the greatest in the history of the game. The field is in a frenzy and the Band can think of no more fitting token than to strike up the Second Movement of the *Supersonic Symphony*, which brings down the other half of the stand.

We're out of the crater but still on the defensive. Unfortunately, it's not been possible to fix Blondin's tight-rope to a strategic point, and he has to find touch. Still, we recover a good bit of ground, and it's a lovely run of Blondin's, especially when you remember that for the last five miles he's being worried by a pack of pterodactyls loosed from a string-bag by a Martian bobby-soxer.

At the line-out it's our ball, but it falls into bad hands. Stavisky catches it and passes it to Bottomley, Bottomley to Jabez Balfour, Jabez Balfour to Charlie Peace, and Charlie Peace to Jonathan Wild, losing ground all the way. Jonathan Wild slings a long one to Judas Iscariot, who sells the pass to the Martian Threequarter line, and they get into their stride. For a surrealist football-fan, no doubt it's a lovely sight to see this far-flung line of giants racing across the jet-black surface of the Moon with the Ball flashing from one wing to the other and back again. For us, who're supposed to stop them, it's slightly different. I'm too busy taking notes of shirkers' names myself, but Engelbrecht insists on showing what he's made of. With a grunt of defiance he hurls himself through the air and catches hold of a Martian Three Q's bootlace. He hangs on like grim death, taking fearful punishment as he's dragged over the lava.

There's nothing to stop them now except Salvador Dalí, our Full Back. Some of us doubt the wisdom of our skipper's

choice of such an *avant-garde* type for such a die-hard position. But we've got to hand it to old Salvador. He tries Everything. As a last attempt to stop them he even camouflages the Goal Posts as a Giant Gallows with some very tasty objects from his studio strung up from the cross-bar. Neither – though some of his less charitable team-mates say this is because he's got stuck in the chest of drawers with which he's been protecting his person – does he flinch from the ultimate sacrifice of a flying tackle. Useless, of course. A brief splintering crash. Then the Martian Three Q touches down between the goal posts.

As we all crowd together in the Goal Mouth there's a multitude of doleful faces such as never was seen since the Last Trump. I've just handed in my list when Charlie Wapentake jogs my arm and points to the Id and Chippy de Zoëte chatting to Pierpoint, the Public Executioner. We know what that means. Somebody's going to swing for it.

The Martians convert and we migrate back to midfield. Soon after the kick-off Vivekananda finds touch. But our luck's out. At the line-out Zerubabel tips it back to Origen, but Origen passes to Julian the Apostate, who starts running back. Luther and John Huss trip him up and start a plucky dribble. They're joined by Calvin who picks up and passes to Wesley. For a glorious moment it looks as if we're

going to get somewhere. Wesley jinks like a rabbit, sells the dummy to three enemy forwards. But he hasn't got the legs. He passes, and one of the Plymouth Brothers knocks on. This time the enemy forwards get the ball and wheel with it. Charlie Marx empties his pistol again and again into the back row of our scrum in an attempt to stop the rot.

10–nil, and the game's only in its first light-year. Some poets start a passing movement. Chatterton passes to Keats, Keats to Shelley, Shelley to Byron, Byron to Wilde, who muffs it. There's a lot of tittering in the loose. The Martians get it back to their Three Q's, and there's no stopping them. They run through us like a dose of salts, cock snooks at the Easter Island statues which Dalí has brought up to guard the Goal Mouth, and score again.

After that it's a procession and they score as they please. Full backs are tried by the dozen only to have rings made round them.

At half-time the score is astronomical, and Wing-forwards are being shot in batches in the Changing Room.

Towards the end of the Interval, Engelbrecht, Lizard Bayliss, his manager, and I, are reclining in our bivouac, toasting our toes at the core of a crater, when Charlie Marx and Fred Engels limp past. 'There's only one way, *knabe,*' we hear Charlie say. 'We must give them the old Trojan horse.' 'All very well,' says

Fred, 'but there's not much room in there.' 'Room for a little 'un,' says Charlie. His eye lights on Engelbrecht. 'How about it, *junge*?' he says, raising an eyebrow and cocking his pistol. 'Care to volunteer for an interesting mission in History's service?' And before we can remonstrate he marches Engelbrecht off to the Changing Room.

We come out for the second half dizzy and defeatist. But the moment they kick off it's clear that a change has come over the game. The Ball is taking a hand. It won't roll right for the Martians nohow. They muff pass after pass and in the scrum our hookers get it every time. It's as if it's grown a little pair of legs of its own. Soon comes our first try. Charlie gathers it clean as a whistle and passes to Fred, who punts for the open field. Stenka Razin and his band trap it and take it on with their feet. There's a fierce loose scrummage in a crater, but Guy Fawkes has got a map of the Underground. The Ball seems to beckon him on. They surface just in front of the Goal, and Jack Cade slips over for a touch-down. Goliath, the new full back, takes the kick. The Ball grazes the cross bar, but instead of bouncing off it seems to hang there in the air. Then it drops over.

The Score is 5,555–5. Things are looking up. The Id commutes the sentences of one in ten of the doomed Wing Forwards to Life in the Scrum. Soon after the kick, Hannibal gets it and blunders right through with his footballing elephants. Goliath converts.

All that epoch the same tactics are repeated. We're using our feet like dancing masters. It's 5,555–5,550 now. Not long to go. Some unlikely characters have scored, even Heliogabalus, Bishop Berkley, and Aubrey Beardsley.

De Mille is looking at his travelling clock. He's lifting the whistle to his lips with both hands. Sorrowfully, Lizard Bayliss folds up the special edition of *The Fly-Paper* with Engelbrecht's Obituary notice, and wipes away a tear. 'If only he could have lived to see this,' he says.

Charlie Marx is giving the forwards their final pep-talk. 'A Spectre is haunting Football!' I hear him bark. 'The time has come to convert the Feet of History into the History of Feet! Forwards of the World! Pack Tight! You have nothing to lose but your Shins!'

The Martians try hard to find touch with a terrific root, but the Ball drops back into play. There follows one of the sweetest pieces of combination in History. Lecky passes to Gibbon, Gibbon to Tacitus, Tacitus to Josephus. Josephus slings a long pass to Isaiah, who punts ahead. Samuel catches it and passes to Lot, Lot to Noah, who gives it to Cain. Cain tries to keep it but it slips sideways out of his fingers. Abel dribbles it over the line and Adam falls flat on it.

Goliath has strained a tendon and the Id orders Dalí out of the Morgue to take the kick. He asks me to place for him.

As he adjusts the angle to his liking I hear Engelbrecht's voice speaking to me from inside the Ball. 'What's the score, chum?' it says. 'I've rather lost count.'

That night, at a little private ceremony in the Changing Room, attended only by Charlie Marx, Arnold of Rugby, and the Politbureau of the Selection Committee, Engelbrecht receives the highest award of Global Football, the crypto-Cap.

As soon as the ceremony is over he's smuggled out of the Changing Room in a tiny coffin.

# 9

# ENGELBRECHT AND THE MECHANICAL BRAIN

*". . . completing her famous boiler dance . . ."*

THE COMMITTEE'S announcement that the Mechanical Brain has been made an honorary member of the Surrealist Sportsman's Club gets rather a mixed reception.

In the vast, cigar-shaped Smoking Room, which is even blacker than usual with the post-prandial fumes of hashish, marijuana, opium, mescal, and other, less homely, narcotics, the gossip is all of the prospective addition to our company.

The opposition is led by two of the oldest members, nicknamed, so as to distinguish them one from another, the Formless Shape and the Shapeless Form. These testy wraiths are quite invisible with indignation at the Committee for not giving them a chance to blackball the monster.

Others, while less intransigent, express apprehension.

'If you ask me,' says Joey De'Ath, pulling hard at a refractory, ether-pickled Elfweed, 'we got quite enough thought-readers in this club already.'

Little Charlie Wapentake, surfacing after a marathon puff at his multiple hubble-bubble, opines sagely: 'Gnash it all, I mean to say, what, he's going to take up the deuce of a lot of room, eh? They say he occupies three floors of the Town Hall.'

And Chippy de Zoëte voices the opinion of the majority when he roars: 'I vote we give the bounder the cold shoulder!' Which, as anyone who has had a peep at Chippy's electro-encephalogram will scarcely need to be told, is more likely to mean the hot foot.

However, as Salvador Dalí never tires of reminding us, the best-laid schemes of mice and Surrealist Sportsmen gang aft agley. When our new honorary member is carried into the Smoking Room, and unpacked and put together by his attendants, he proves so nippy at anticipating Chippy's practical jokes – always knowing exactly where in the carpet the forest fire is going to break out, which chandeliers have been timed to go off as catherine wheels and which to rain down assegais – and takes them all in such good part, that before long he has become the most popular member in the club. His dials are thronged from Dreamtime to Coma with Surrealist Sportsmen, eager to chew the fat with him, and perhaps pick up a tip for some forthcoming cosmic event. Every now and again, such is the spell of the Mechanical Brain's captivating personality, they burst into: 'For he's a jolly good entity! And so say all of us!'

Into this atmosphere of peace and goodwill to all thought-forms enters my friend Engelbrecht, the dwarf surrealist boxer, fresh from a tour of the Welsh holiday resorts, where he has been giving a series of exhibition bouts with a punch-drunk dentist's chair who fights under the name of Casse Noisette.

Some of us have figured that Engelbrecht's experiences in the ring, knocking the dials off clocks and eviscerating

slot machines with right hooks to the works, will not be such as to endear him to a Mechanical Brain, and mischiefmakers have hopes of promoting an unseemly fracas in the Smoking Room.

But no sooner does the Mechanical Brain catch on to Engelbrecht's wavelength than all the dials start purring at once and he registers the maximum degree of pleasure possible. From then on he and the dwarf are inseparable.

Towards the end of the Epoch, at the season of celebration and regret, the Club Committee announce a special dinner in honour of the Mechanical Brain at which full clock-work will be worn. This time there is not a dissident voice, and everything looks to be all set for one of the most festive evenings in Surrealist Sporting history.

Dinner, which is held in a private room at the Power Station, is the devil of a do. The Mechanical Brain sits between the Id and Engelbrecht, and he's so happy he gives out a continuous crackle of blue sparks. His diet is a bit *recherché*, consisting mainly of curves and measurements, but his attendants have done their best to fix him a really slap-up meal. Once the crackle becomes a roar, and I gather that the MB is laughing at a rather esoteric joke about the difference between the co-ordinates for a 4-dimensional sirloin and a bathing beauty's hip.

At last Dreamy Dan, our Surrealist Toastmaster, pronounces the time-honoured formula: 'Gentlemen, you may drug.' Opium pipes and reefers are lit; ether sprays are squirted; and we wind up our main springs, oil our cogs, and get set for the speeches.

I won't bother you with all that is said, but so fervent and sincere are the tributes paid to the Mechanical Brain that when the time comes for him to reply he is overcome with Purpose Tremor (which is a complaint that Mechanical Brains suffer from in moments of stress) and unable to utter so much as a spark.

It's a heartrending time for us, as the attendants – electronic engineers, statisticians and cybernetecists – fuss round his dial and coils, adjusting and computing until they get him on the beam again. Then he thanks us very prettily and, by way of an after-dinner story, proceeds to recite the contents of the 'case' books in the British Museum Library – those which are kept under lock and key and can only be read, by special permission, in the North Library.

By now we are well on in the seventh stage of intoxication. The weaker brethren have been carried away, some by the men in white, others by indescribable phantasms of their own imagining. Only the tough inner cadre of Surrealist Sport remains, grouped round the guest of honour, plying him with the formulae for vegetable alkaloids, which he seems well able to take.

Joey De'Ath exhales lightly, and the last of the MB's attendants to retain any shreds of the priceless gift of consciousness rolls over on his back, flat out as a slide-rule.

With a high-pitched sound like a schoolgirl's giggle the Mechanical Brain emits a stream of violent sparks. Engelbrecht leaps on the table to address the company.

His proposal is simplicity itself. Nothing more than to give the Mechanical Brain a bit of fun, take him out and show him some mechanical night life, free him for a few glorious hours from the irksome restraint of the laboratory.

There is tremendous enthusiasm for this humane, machine proposal, and in less time than it takes to tell, the MB – with Engelbrecht and Dr Sadismus, the Surrealist Surgeon (who has just popped in after a difficult delivery at the Clock Hospital) at the controls – is being borne by a forest of willing hands, fins, tentacles and other appendages belonging to a host of Surrealist sons of Belial, whooping and shrieking through the streets of Night-town, *en route* for the red light district down by the marshalling yard.

OUR first port of call is Puffing Billy's, a notorious haunt of dissolute locomotives. We arrive in the middle of the cabaret just as La Donkey Engine is completing her famous boiler dance. Puffing Billy ushers us to a table near the floor and whistles up a bevy of his most glamorous hostesses – pressure-gauges and cash registers – to keep us entertained.

Soon they are clustered round the Mechanical Brain like odalisques in a seraglio. And all the time they're ticking up the dollars. It seems they're built to measure every amorous impulse transmitted by the customer's works, and our guest of the evening has a no end friendly disposition. The last thing in the world we want is to embarrass the old dear, but it looks like our bill is going to be astronomical, so Engelbrecht chugs over for a quiet word with Puffing Billy to ask him to have mercy on us.

I don't know quite how it starts, but suddenly there is a piercing whistle followed by clouds of steam and the next thing we see is Engelbrecht knocking the bogie wheels from under Puffing Billy.

It's a cheerful little rough house while it lasts, but as soon as Puffing Billy's chuckers-out – two plug-ugly Bull-dozers and a Steam-shovel – come into action it's all over, and we find ourselves out on our ears in the marshalling yard, all among the burdock, the coal dust, the granite chips, and the tarred sleepers. The Mechanical Brain seems rather the worse for wear, but Engelbrecht and Dr Sadismus give him some first-aid shock treatment with a live rail, which makes him so frisky again that he clamours persistently to go on somewhere else.

I must say I've no idea the Night Life of the Machine World is so elaborate. My recollections of the rest of the evening are a trifle blurred, but I distinctly remember being asked to leave 'Pi' because Chippy de Zoëte will keep peering under a young racing car's bonnet. I am certainly present when we wreck *The Needy Knife Grinder*, a pretentious mechanical *boîte* with an early industrial revolution period décor, and a very equivocal clientèle. But after this I become disoriented, and – though I am told later that I do my best to save poor little Charlie Wapentake from the frightful fate that overtakes him at *The Saw Mill* – I do not surface again until we are being shown to our table in *The Precision Tool Room*.

This is a terrifically tony, upstage joint, a haunt of the Greenwich Observatory Chronometer and Instruments from the National Physical Laboratory. I'm very surprised they let us in, especially as Chippy de Zoëte makes what I can only describe as a mechanically criminal assault on the photo-electric apparatus on duty in the cloakroom. His apology – that he thinks it is a hat check girl – is hardly likely to heal the breach.

But in we go, and the first thing we see is a large party of Precision types from the Nat Phys Lab escorted by some Range-finders and Geiger counters in uniform. The atmosphere is so overwhelmingly correct that anybody would think they were at the 400 on a night when the princesses have dropped in and there's been a directive from the palace against dancing cheek to cheek.

And now the effects of all the insidious stuff he's been downing at last begin to tell on our guest of the evening. He develops a most disturbing form of machine's megalomania, starts sending out ugly looking red waves and bawls at the top of his sound-box that he intends to enforce the good old mechanical tradition of the *droit du seigneur*, and will all machines present in *The Precision Tool Room* come over at once to our table and pay him homage. He makes it pretty clear what he means by homage.

The management of *The Precision Tool Room* have already threatened to cut the power off if we don't pull ourselves together, but Joey De'Ath and the Formless Shape and the Shapeless Form degauss the chuckers-out and mount guard over the switch-board.

It looks as if we're in for a horrible orgy. But a deputation from their table consisting of the senior Range-finder, a Geiger counter, and something very diaphanous from the Nat Phys Lab, come over to us and start lecturing the Mechanical Brain for all they're worth. It sounds like a sarcastic headmaster tongue lashing the lower fifth. They end up by telling him he's a disgrace to electronic engineering and ought to be thoroughly ashamed of himself and go home to bed.

I don't know how it is but their remarks go straight to the heart of the Mechanical Brain. There is a crackle of sparks followed by a terrible howling noise. Then he switches over to the most deplorable crying jag you ever witnessed. What's more, the black waves he emits turn out to be highly infectious and in no time at all the entire party of us are prostrate with melancholia.

You can hear the sobs and guilt-stricken lamentations all over Night-town. The Manager of *The Precision Tool Room* sends for a Breakdown Gang and we are taken away under care.

And so this once hilarious night out draws to its gloomy close. It takes us some æons to recover from this hangover, and the last we hear of the Mechanical Brain he is only able to earn a bare pittance in a penny bank, doing very simple addition, hand-operated.

# 10

# DIRTY WORK AT THE DOGS' OPERA

*". . . beating time with a tuning fork . . ."*

WE HAVE never suspected our friend, Engelbrecht, the dwarf surrealist boxer, of harbouring an æsthetic conscience. The news, therefore, that he is undertaking to finance a Season of Song at the Old Dogs' Opera House causes quite a furore in the Dream Room of the Surrealist Sportsman's Club.

There is much cynical comment on the unwisdom of a tone-deaf dwarf setting up as Butter-and-Egg-Man to Bulldogs and Angel to Aberdeens. Then I hear the foggy voice of Chippy de Zoëte laying five to two 'in anything you like, Space, Time, or Pleasurable Sensations', that the curtain will never rise again after the opening night.

To me, knowing Chippy's form as a saboteur, this bodes little good to my friend's cultural enterprise, and it is with a heavy heart that I listen presently to a message transmitted by the Club's dumb waiter, whose telepathic gift enables us to dispense with a telephone, from Engelbrecht's pessimistic manager, Lizard Bayliss.

'You got to help us, chum,' he quavers. 'We're counting on you for Deputy Wardrobe Master and Second Prompter. For Dog's sake come over quick. Ouch! Down! You brutes! Down, I say.' The rest is drowned in a chorus of baying and howling that sounds like a meet of the Baskerville.

The Old Dogs' Opera House, designed by the brothers Landseer, whose portraits of celebrated canine Thespians adorn the foyer and green-room, is a vast, kennel-shaped edifice that would make the Crystal Palace look like a mouse-trap. It's fallen into desuetude this long time, not from any shortage of talent but from lack of patronage.

You see, Dogs' Opera is big stuff; much bigger than Grand Opera. There's only one work in the repertoire. It's just called *The Dogs' Opera*. But it's got everything. It makes *The Ring* seem like one of Gertrude Jennings' curtain-raisers.

When I arrive, Engelbrecht is standing on top of a kennel the size of Noah's Ark, beating time with a tuning fork with a lash tied to the end of it, while the bloodhound who sings the leading role of Fido tries out his famous aria, *Semper Fidelis.*

Meanwhile, in a clearing in a forest way down stage, Lizard Bayliss, wearing one of those padded outfits they use for police dog trials, is rehearsing the Drinking Chorus.

'Call yourselves a Dogs' Voice Choir?' he is sneering. 'Why, a scratch mob from Battersea could sing better than that. Now we'll start all over again. The St Bernards with the brandy barrels come on from the OP side and fill the drinking bowls. Look at me, if you please, Towser, not at the scenery. Yes, it's quite real but all the rabbits have been netted. Then the rest of you start quaffing, I mean lapping, like beggary. No, not now, Rover, you chump. Wait for it. Those who don't know their words can wuff 'em.'

With that he cracks his whip and they all give tongue:

*Here's to the Basset of bashful fifteen*
*And here's to the Dachshund of fifty.*

It sounded a bit cracked to me but I'm not used to the canine voice.

Lizard Bayliss seems as pleased as Punch. 'Much more like it, dogs,' he says. 'A very nice piece of vocalizing. Trot off to your kennels now and all be back here at nine sharp. Poodles in practice dress. We'll try the *Lament for Waldmann* from Act One, Scene Fifty-six. You can't go wrong on that. It's straight howling. I'll just refresh your memories. The veteran hound, Waldmann, has eaten the poisoned ragoût intended for Fido. He's lying dead in mid-stage with his paws folded. Fido enters and sniffs him. And mind you lie still, Waldmann. No irreverent twitching. Fido sings a long aria extolling the virtues of his dead friend. Towards its close the Dogs' Voice Choir come softly on. Softly, I said, Rover, so get your claws clipped. It's a sad scene, this, and we don't want it spoiled by a ruddy tap dance...'

Everything seems to me to be going a lot better than could be expected and it begins to look as if Chippy de Zoëte may drop a packet. Fido strolls over with Engelbrecht on his shoulder, and they take me on a tour of the stars' dressing kennels. I'm introduced to a ravishing little soubrette, a white poodle who sings Poupee, the diseuse at the dogs' *café chantant* where Fido gets taken on as chucker-out in Act Two. Also to Dido, the heroine, a temperamental Great Dane with a rich, creamy, stableyard contralto.

Although she's heroine it's not much of a part. She gets dog-napped early in the plot and is chained up off-stage for ages. I can see there's no love lost between her and Poupée, and Lizard Bayliss tells me it's a job to keep her from chawing the plucky little artiste right up.

She's equally jealous of the Red Setter – a gloriously regal looking lady-dog she is too – who sings Flavia, the Queen of the Coverts, and tries to corrupt Fido's integrity in a long aria, *All This To Thee I Promise*, about the allure of smart dogs' life in a gunroom de luxe and his photograph in the *Catler* and the *Bitch*.

I also met Cavaliere Craporello, the canine Toscanini, whom Engelbrecht has imported from the Isle of Dogs to conduct the Canine Symphony Orchestra.

From now on life is the usual backstage whirl with a fresh crisis breaking every hour. I'm taken off prompting because a lot of the libretto is in Latin and these dogs are so smart they all use the new pronunciation. But I find my level as Deputy Keeper of the Chorus Dogs' Boots and Spurs and general man's body…

With his usual crazy optimism Engelbrecht hasn't allowed us half enough time to rehearse and before we know where we are the First Night is upon us.

Our temperamental cast gets worse jitters than any of the clientèle of the Ivy, and the Opera House Vet has his hands full. Dido throws a howling fit. Poupée complains that Flavia has pupped on her ball-dress. Fido's swallowed a swarm of flies and we have to spray his throat with Flit. And the old

THE CANINE DIVA

After Edwin Landseer

*Now hanging in the Green Room*
*at the Dog's Opera House*

Airedale who plays the Fairy Fustypaws in the prologue is stuck in a rabbit hole up-stage.

But somehow we get them all sorted out in time and I hear the Call-pup yapping along the corridors: 'Prologue and Act One, Scene One. Beginners please.'

We've been on the alert for sabotage all through rehearsals, of course, with strict screening of visitors and man-traps outside the stars' dressing kennels; but nary a bite except one poor old stage-door-Johnnie delivering fan-mail. Our information is that Chippy de Zoëte is saving his effort for the opening night. And if the butchers' vans in front of the stage door mean what I think they mean, it's going to be a whale of an effort.

However, I have every confidence in Bowser and Bawsie, our stagedoor-keepers, two old mastiffs who used to sing in Dogs' Opera themselves before they lost their voices. They may be *passé* but they know, none better, the rule of the Opera House: '*No bouquets of meat, bones, or offal to be delivered to artistes, whether on the stage or in their dressing kennels, until after the final curtain.*'

The Overture to the Dogs' Opera is a full-bodied composition. As the music critic of *The Fly-Paper* says, it makes Tchaikovski's *1812* sound like Berners' *Lullaby for a New-Born Gnat*. Craporello complains he's never been able to rehearse it properly because Engelbrecht is so stingy with the gunpowder. Nevertheless, he gets some wonderful chords out of those massed cannon and cathedral chimes. Several times he's blasted right off his rostrum into the orchestra pit, only to bound back, nonchalantly fitting a fresh rocket to his baton.

Meanwhile, through the billowing clouds of smoke, steam, and sound, I glimpse row upon row of immaculate Dogs' Opera-goers packing the stalls – and the Id, and his party of surrealist socialites Tommy Prenderghast, Monkey Trevelyan, Bones Barlow, Nodder Fothergill, Willy Warlock, Joey De'Ath, and scores more, making mayhem in the immensity of the Stage-Box.

Little Charlie Wapentake, who's acting as my tip-off, starts to tic-tac a message, but just then there's some more heavy percussion and when the smoke clears away poor Charlie is no longer in possession of the priceless gift of consciousness, one of his cronies having crowned him with a heavy Cr 8vo volume containing the programme.

The Prologue is a formidable Epos in Dog-Latin, High German, Old and Middle English, liberally spiced with Sanscrit *doubles entendres*. But the Fairy Fustypaws never falters. All her training at the Comédie Canine comes to her aid and she holds that difficult, mixed audience spellbound by faultless declamation and brilliant miming. You'd never guess that a little while back she was drawing blood from her dressers as they plucked the burrs off her coat.

The curtain rises on Scene One, with its slangily provocative Huntsman's Chorus:

*D'ye ken John Peel?*
*He's a dog-gone heel.*

and the first Act goes off without serious mishap. There's one awkward moment in the Duel Scene when Fido gets his sword stuck in a tree, and can't get it out again, though he grunts and tugs at the hilt with his teeth like billyo.

The hidden hand of Chippy de Zoëte is long delayed, but when it strikes it strikes hard. Scene 56 of Act 4 is one of the biggest in the entire opus. Fido, our hero, wrongfully certified through the machinations of his enemy, the wolfhound, Masterman (by Moriarty out of Messalina, and a stupendous basso profundo), has fetched up in the refractory mental ward of the Royal Veterinary College. He is acting hysterically owing to the drug which Masterman put in his drinking trough, and is suspected of rabies. But he recovers his sanity just in time, joins forces with one of the other inmates, a deluded wirehaired terrier, known by his asylum sobriquet of the Mad Dog Rags, and organizes a break out. The scene, which is painful and moving in the extreme, closes with the stirring and thunderous March of the Mad Dogs – on Buckingham Palace.

It is halfway through, and the stage is in darkness. I am keeping an eye on the Rovers – mostly collies – at the back of the Dress Circle, when I get a message to report backstage.

I don't recognize Engelbrecht at first; he's dressed as a Yorkshire terrier. 'Hop into this, chum,' he says, holding out a dog-skin and mask, 'and get down on all fours. We're wanted on the stage. Under cover of darkness de Zoëte's loosed the population of the Good Samaritan Cats' Home on us.'

By the time we've rounded up the last cat, and Lizard and I have rescued Engelbrecht from the back row of the Dogs' Voice Choir, who are worrying him like a hearthrug, the curtain is ready to go up again. For several scenes after this the performance is very ragged indeed, and the Cavaliere Craporello more than once exchanges the baton for the whip.

Then just as the cast are beginning to settle down again Chippy de Zoëte plays his final coup. He infiltrates into the

cast, via a tunnel in the Fairy Fustypaws' dressing kennel, a band of desperate ruffians from the condemned kennel at Battersea.

They dognap Fido, and one of them changes into his costume for the next scene – a tender passage between hero and heroine, which this villainous pseudo-Fido has been ordered to wreck by clowning in the lowest imaginable fashion, like any street cur round a lamp-post. It will spell the end of Dogs' Opera for some time to come and we are powerless to prevent it because all three of us have been dognapped, muzzled and kennelled, in full view of the stage.

The curtain rises to reveal the Dogs' Voice Choir, one of whom is already so demoralized he's chewing a string of sausages, dressed as Philosopher Kings, discussing, in strophe and anti-strophe, the Good, the True and the Beautiful. Dido enters, attended by a train of wise virgin spaniels.

Horror-struck – for we have been told what is afoot – we watch the pseudo-Fido waiting in the wings for his cue.

He quaffs a final Dog's Nose proffered by his unsuspecting dresser, and bounds on-stage.

But as the orchestra strikes up, a mysterious change comes over him. For a moment he looks as if he's going to howl. And then, true as a bell, from his poor mangy throat, come the strains of *Semper Fidelis*.

Afterwards we learn that the pseudo-Fido used to be a famous tenor himself until he lost his voice and went right down in the world. The opening bars of *Semper Fidelis* bring it back again. So, instead of clowning bestially, he sings the part straight, though he knows full well that by breaking his sabotage contract with Chippy he's heading straight back for Battersea.

After that it's a regular bow wow wow. The rest of the cast are electrified and the performance of the last seven acts reaches classic heights. Never, as *The Fly-Paper*'s music critic says, as he helps himself to my glass of mead at the party afterwards, never have such unearthly strains been heard. Engelbrecht does a fizzing deal with the libraries and Chippy de Zoëte has to sell his dreams to pay his debts.

# 11

# ENGELBRECHT, M.P.

*". . . they soon clear the Square with their broomsticks . . ."*

Now that the Race has run its course, and we exist but as whispers in the Void, I feel the time has come for me to lift the veil which has hitherto shrouded the parliamentary candidature of my friend Engelbrecht, the dwarf surrealist boxer.

For me, the story begins early one manic-depressive cycle, not long after the celebrations that followed – rather tastelessly, some thought – the collapse of the Moon . . .

I am lolling at ease on my cosy, red rubber-covered surgical couch in the Convulsion Room at the Surrealist Sportsman's Club, watching the antics of poor little Charlie Wapentake. He has just regurgitated his gag and is endeavouring to spell out the leading article in *The Fly-Paper*, when invitation placards are wheeled in from the Id, that veteran patron of Surrealist Sport, bidding us to a week-end of mixed electioneering at Nightmare Abbey.

We are no end vexed at such short notice.

'Impossible,' I say. 'I'm suiciding with Lamia at the Necropole. She'll never forgive me if I throw her over.'

'And I'm gnashed if I'm going to let little Bonzo de Sousa down,' cries Charlie staunchly. 'We're having fits together at Cruft's.'

But an invitation from the Id is a Royal Command, and when, at 00.00 hours, the Town Drain glides into Platform N at the Infinite Terminus, there we are, milling for seats with the rest of the Surrealist Fancy, including Engelbrecht. The loquacious dwarf has brought a telescopic speakers' platform from which he treats us all to an impromptu address of extracts from Bradshaw and Cruden's Concordance – much to the disgust of his pessimistic manager, Lizard Bayliss.

'I dunno what's come over the little beezer,' mutters this worthy. 'He's been talking nineteen to the dozen, any words he can get his tongue around, ever since he got the invite. Mixed electioneering indeed! It's breaking training, that's what it is. What sort of shape will he be in when the time comes for him to step into Parliament Square for his bout with Big Ben?'

*En route* for Nightmare, Nodder Fothergill puts me in the political picture. The rural constituency of Monkslust, in which the Abbey stands, is a rotten borough in the gift of the Id's family. Young Unconscious, the last holder of the seat, has two heads, and in the middle of his maiden speech, shortly before the liquidation of parliament, one of these heads interrupts the other and refuses to accept the Shrieker's directive to pipe down. After this the Surrealist Party Flagellators decide that another and better integrated candidate is needed.

There is no time to be lost. On arrival at the Abbey, the rafters of the Great Oubliette are swept for informers. Then the nitrous oxide taps are turned on and our Convention gets down to business.

A move to adopt Bones Barlow, the Master of the Man-hunt and a wholesomely nightmarish type thought suitable for a rural constituency, is blocked by Monkey Trevelyan, the Id's

agent, who points out that the peasantry hold Bones in some abhorrence as a Ghoul. Charlie Wapentake, though a local boy and beautifully bred, is insufficiently responsible; an offer by Dr Sadismus to stabilize him then and there by pre-frontal lobotomy is declined with thanks. Discussion ranges from this character to that. Some are too old; some are too bad; some are too mad. And Salvador Dalí is disqualified on grounds of nationality. In the end the nomination goes to Engelbrecht.

Monkey Trevelyan warns us against anything too extreme, and for his first manifesto Engelbrecht is content to promise two days off the working week, and one hour on to the Ecstasy. His foreign policy he takes direct from Edward III: the invasion of France. He adds, when it is pointed out to him that he is neglecting the unmarried woman's Vote, the Repeal of the Laws against Witchcraft.

It is, as Nodder Fothergill opines, a modest little programme with something for everyone, and when our candidate proclaims it, without a murmur of dissent, at his first meeting in the boundless wastes of the Market Square at Monkslust, to an audience of grinning cobblestones, who have been well soused with rum by the council's water carts, his election is thought to be in the bag – if only we can get someone to vote for him.

But no sooner do we start canvassing than we encounter a strange current of hostility towards us and our Party. It starts in a particularly remote and backward district where poor little Charlie Wapentake is brutally assaulted by a scarecrow whose vote he has solicited in all good faith. Nodder and I are sent out to bring in his remains, and when, after a stiff rearguard action, we fight our way back to the Abbey, we find a scene of dismay and confusion. Reports coming through to HQ, where the Id's Grandmother is on duty at the Witch Ball, indicate that a reign of terror is raging.

Everything and everyone is against us. Joey De'Ath, addressing a meeting of cottage furniture in a tea shop named Ye Wee Waif, and thought to be an absolutely safe locale, is heckled by a Welsh Dresser and set upon by a pair of Wheel Backs. Bones Barlow, gallantly canvassing the wildest of the Women's Institutes disguised as a *sage femme*, gets recognized and narrowly escapes being hatpinned to the notice board. Rollo Chatteridge, leafletizing the churchyard, is upended by a tombstone; and Crabs Felkin, attempting to put a public opinion poll to an Almshouse, is done dark brown by a poisoned wig.

We are bitterly counting our losses when Engelbrecht himself arrives – carried in on a stretcher.

'The dwarf's been KO'd by a gipsy's baby,' gulps Lizard Bayliss between his sobs. 'We was winding up a meeting on Gallows Common, where the Condemned Dwellings are, and he starts kissing the babies same as Monkey Trevelyan tells him to, and this little perisher crowns him. It's the first time he's been KO'd since he was fouled in the Aura by a Nasmyth Hammer at Woolwich Arsenal. God blow me tight! Crowned by a crêche! If *The Fly-Paper* gets to hear of this the Kid's reputation is ruined.'

'*A trois pas! Tirez aux Mouches!*' yells Tommy Prenderghast, who is still a bit concussed by a mammet, hurled by some unconvinced villein.

Engelbrecht is not one to take this kind of thing lying down. As soon as he has recovered the priceless gift of consciousness, he tells us to summon a monster mass meeting right away, and see that Market Square is packed, no matter what we have to do to pack it, and even if it's only packed with monsters…

Well, of course, there's only one way to pack the Square and that's to call out the Man-Hunt. Bones Barlow dons his Death's Head, lets loose the Baskerville Breed, and draws that Rotten Borough from Gallows Wood to Witches' Wen.

The Square is packed all right, though if I were to tell you all it's packed with you wouldn't sleep for a week. Take it from me there's no space to squeeze in another succubus.

Engelbrecht climbs the steps to the rostrum. 'My friends,' he says, and pauses to let that sink in because a good many of his audience have never been called 'friends' before. Then he repeats the word, rolling the R so they shan't mistake it for 'fiends'. 'My friends,' he says, 'I'm not going to make a lot of lying electioneering promises which I shall never be able to keep. I'm not here to bulldoze you. I'm here to get elected. My policy is a simple one. Vote for me and I promise you eternal life for all…'

He pauses again, thinking that will knock them, and we members of the committee nudge each other in anticipation of the roar of applause.

But instead of applause there is a storm of heckling: 'What standard of life?' 'With or without Cripps?' 'Will there be flesh-rationing?' 'How about free false fangs for werewolves?'

In vain does Engelbrecht roar that the standard of life will be the highest imaginable. The hail of questions becomes a storm of booing. Finally the Id has to close the meeting by ringing the dread tocsin on the Abbey Bell.

'Well,' says Nodder Fothergill, as we troop back disconsolate, 'there seems to be no satisfying those buzzards. If you ask me they've been got at.'

Monkey Trevelyan shakes his palsied head. 'Much better have stuck to the old programme,' he says. 'At least we should have been certain of the Witches' vote.'

At this rate it looks as if the valuable Deposit, which the Id has been storing up, will be forfeit.

But at dinner this night – a scratch meal of cold vampire bats – little Charlie Wapentake has the one brain-wave of his life. Looking down the rows of gloomy faces he says: 'I say, gnash it all, what's become of Chippy de Zoëte? I don't seem to have seen him for ages.'

And at once everything becomes clear to us. Plain old-fashioned sabotage is our trouble. With Chippy de Zoëte and his gang of doppelgangers spreading alternate slanders and fantasies throughout the constituency it's no wonder we've been unable to canvass a vote.

The position seems hopeless. De Zoëte has got such a start on us that whatever we can think up in the way of a programme he's bound to beat us to the punch. Engelbrecht is all for a straight fight, but how?

We're just going to turn it in when Monkey Trevelyan asks for the floor. 'There's one way and one only of swinging this election,' he says, wagging his sage old poll. 'We must drop all our fancy programmes and go bald-headed for the Witches' vote. There's enough witches in this constituency to elect a whole parliament.'

'But, Monkey,' says Nodder, 'how do you suppose we're going to persuade the local Witches to vote for the Id's candidate when it's well known the Id's the keenest Witch-shooter in the shire?'

'There's only one way,' says Monkey Trevelyan. 'The Id must sign a Covenant abrogating his Witch-shooting rights.'

All eyes turn to the head of the table where the old Id is sitting concealed behind a cloud of smoke.

It goes against the grain, of course, but there's nothing else to be done. The Id's Grandmother gets through to the Chief Witch on her Witch Ball and presently she drops in to draw up the terms. The Id tries to persuade her that shooting Witches is the best way of preserving them and suggests he should keep the rights of Gallows Wood, but she's not having any.

At last, it's all signed and delivered, but Monkey Trevelyan thinks we should do a spot of canvassing to keep our constituents up to the mark. Engelbrecht, plucky as ever, thinks nothing of kissing Witches all round the clock, but Lizard Bayliss is so scared he goes to ground in Father Carfax's – the Id's Chaplain's – cassock, and we have to send imps down to get him out.

What with guarding our little candidate in case the Witches take too strong a fancy to him, and protecting the electorate against intimidation by Chippy de Zoëte, we have our hands full. Comes Polling Day, and Nodder Fothergill and I are posted on top of the Obelisk on Gallows Common to flag the Witches in through Chippy's barrage balloons which he has adorned with biblical texts such as 'Thou Shalt Not Suffer A Witch to Vote', but we guide them all through; they touch down at the Polling Booth in Market Square. There's a bit of a dust-up with the opposition but they soon clear the Square with their broomsticks. Engelbrecht gets in unopposed and is chaired all over the square in a ducking stool.

When the result is announced, Chippy de Zoëte breaks down and confesses that he is being blackmailed by an owl which read his night thoughts. But just what he was promising the electorate we can never quite make out.

The opening of Parliament is fixed for the same day as Engelbrecht's fight with Big Ben and the sky over Parliament Square is thick with constituents, waiting to cheer their candidate.

But the fight never takes place and Engelbrecht never takes his seat. Big Ben lodges a protest with the Referee that there are Witches in his works. The Ref says 'So what?,' but Big Ben's hands start turning backwards so fast that soon we're back in the days of the Long Parliament and the Rump, followed by the Witenagemot, and before we know where we are there's nothing in the Square except a tree and some apes squabbling over a groundnut, and soon after that nothing at all.

# 12

# ENGELBRECHT'S ELOPEMENT

*". . . Faint heart never won fair Chronometer . . ."*

DESPITE OUR seeming remoteness from the World of Everyday, there are signs by which we members of the Surrealist Sportsman's Club seldom fail to recognize the arrival of Spring.

Among these harbingers are natural phenomena, such as the budding of the Upas tree in our secretary's buttonhole, the proliferation of Dead Men's Fingers in the chef's Electric Eel tank, and the appearance of cactus spikes round the edges of that Desert of Vast Eternity optimistically known as the Smoking Room carpet.

These latter are sown regularly by the Oldest Member, an inveterate sentimentalist and one of the most avid gluttons for punishment in the history of matrimony. He sows them, so he tells us, in memory of his twenty-fifth wife, 'my poor little Gagool…'

It is one green gloaming, well on in the tender season, and a knot of us are reclining dreamily round the Witch Ball in the Wish Fulfilment Room.

The air is thick with romance. Presently little Charlie Wapentake breaks the silence with a sigh so deep that we have to fasten our safety belts to save ourselves from being sucked in.

'Cough it up, Charlie boy,' says Chippy de Zoëte, a trifle coarsely. 'What's it this time? Animal? Vegetable? Mineral? Or Abstract?'

And it doesn't take us twenty questions to find out that our susceptible fellow member has lost his heart to Good Queen Mary's Galoshes.

A round of confessions follows and some winsome object choices are revealed.

Nodder Fothergill is head over heels in love with St Pancras Station. Joey De'Ath is crazy, but crazy, about the Iron Maiden of Nuremberg. Bones Barlow is clean gone on the Shot Tower. Monkey Trevelyan is threatening to handcuff himself to the Black Maria's bonnet. Tommy Prenderghast has popped the question to the 'Pru. Salvador Dalí has made suggestions to Smithfield Meat Market, though how he imagines that even he is going to fit it into a bijou love nest in St John's Wood is more than even we can figure out. As for Badger Norridge, he admits what we have known all along: that he is wedded to his opium Pipe.

After suitable toasts have been suitably drunk to our respective fetishes, we break, in chorus, into the well-known Surrealist Love Song:

*I love it! I love it! And who shall dare*
*To chide me for loving my grandmother's chair?*

which, as the company does not fail to point out, is all the more poignant in my case, because my grandfather was a dentist.

We have just lowered the floor with this ditty when in strolls my friend Engelbrecht, the dwarf surrealist boxer, accompanied by his pessimistic manager, Lizard Bayliss.

I can tell at once, from the edgy way Lizard snaps at the Editor of *The Fly-Paper*, who waltzes past just then, that something is up. Disentangling myself from the Oldest Member, who has gaffed me in the buttonhole the better to drool to me of his boyhood romance with Judith Malmains, the Plague Nurse, I hurry over.

'I tell you, kiddo,' Lizard is saying, 'you can't go through with it. It spells ruin for the pair of you.'

Engelbrecht ignores him. There is an expression of dreamy bliss on the dwarf's rubbery mug. He keeps on humming: 'I love it! I love it! And who shall dare!'

'Dare, indeed,' snorts Lizard. 'He'll do you both to rights. That's what he'll dare.' He turns to me. 'He's going to elope with Grandfather Clock's grand-daughter, Cuckoo,' he whispers. 'I tell him not over my watch-chain, he ain't.'

I can well understand the faithful impresario's trepidation. Ever since Engelbrecht's sensational defeat of Grandfather Clock in their famous ten-round contest, his relations with all timepieces have been atrocious. The danger, therefore, of gang-work, of every conceivable kind, including the metaphysical, is too plain.

However, there is no stopping Engelbrecht. And we, his fellow members, true to the principle that all the world loves a lover, feel compelled to rally round and lend at least – as Badger Norridge wittily puts it – a minute hand.

The set-up is not altogether unfavourable. Grandfather Clock, accompanied by his grand-daughter, Cuckoo, is spending the week-end at Greenwich Observatory as guest of the Chronometer Royal. It's a rather special house party in celebration of the Vernal Equinox, and the guests include some very distinguished dials, among them Big Ben, the BBC Time Pips, and a Roman Water Clock from the Museum at St Albans.

Our plan is to infiltrate downstream, disguised as a party of marines escorting the Nautical Almanac, and, at the height of the festivities, during the Dance of the Hours, for Engelbrecht to nip ashore and carry off his prize. Father Carfax, the Id's rascally Chaplain, undertakes to marry them secretly in the little Wristlet-Chapel of Watchmaker's Hall, so that the runaway match shall be instantaneously regularized.

We get our final briefing at a tense meeting in the Trance Room. Lizard Bayliss, looking like a shadow of himself, owing to worry, goes round with his calendar, collecting the hours that will be needed to bribe the Alarm Clocks which the Special Chronological Branch have posted round the Observatory. Everybody gives him something. The Id, who is practically timeless, anyway, and can well afford it, comes through handsomely with a Light Year. Even the Oldest Member, who's not got long to go, coughs up a wheezy five minutes.

At last everything is ready. I have been assigned to the forrard landing party which is to cover Engelbrecht's retreat. But no sooner do we arrive at the Robert Vick than we discover that all our watches have stopped and none of us can remember the date. Sabotage is suspected. Chippy de Zoëte, grilled by Dr Sadismus, breaks down and confesses he has sold our plans to the TIMe Signal at his local telephone exchange for the promise of a Leap Year.

With the element of surprise removed our chances of success have greatly diminished. Some of us, and especially Lizard Bayliss, are for turning back, but Engelbrecht is determined to proceed. He rallies us to him by apt quotation of the old adage: 'Faint heart never won fair Chronometer.' We improvise a pendulum by suspending Chippy de Zoëte from a post of vantage, and rig up an hour-glass with a handful of Wally Warlock's loose teeth. Then we bend to the oars.

A full account of the tricks which those cunning clocks play on us would take me into abstruse realms of physics and philosophy. As little Charlie Wapentake says, 'It's bad enough not knowing where you are, but not knowing when's the very devil.'

Soon after the start, Lizard Bayliss, who is the look-out man, emits a fearful, if correctly nautical, cry of 'Horror on the port bow!' and falls overboard.

We look where he indicates and see ourselves on the way back, deplorably aged and much changed for the worse in every respect. We are followed immediately by Ourselves as We Might Have Been if only we hadn't wasted so much Time.

This is dismal enough but there is plenty more to come. Somehow they have got at our works so that our rhythms and rates of growth are all different. Thus it takes Nodder Fothergill, who is rowing stroke, the best part of a week to clear his throat, while Badger Norridge, at bow, has brought up and reared a family before you can say Jack Ratcatcher. Some of us seem to be growing younger and some older, all at the same time, and what with school caps here, and skull caps there, it really is all very confusing indeed.

By the time we arrive at the point of disembarkation we are utterly disoriented, and the landing party that follows Engelbrecht ashore appears to consist of a brace of toddlers, three dotards, and something that looks as if it died a very long time ago, which we identify, from its expression of extreme dejection, as Lizard Bayliss. Before we can move a

step we have to expend all our precious hoard of contributed Hours, intended for bribing the alarm clocks, on restoring ourselves to some semblance of vitality.

The Dance of the Hours is at its height. The Whittington Chimes are getting ready to swing their introduction to the dread Zero, as we file through the gate into the Astronomer Royal's private garden. Miss Cuckoo Clock, a very sizable model, is waiting for her lover beside the historic sundial. She's ticking away like mad.

Engelbrecht steps forward to claim her and all the alarm clocks planted by the Special Chronological Branch, who've been revelling on borrowed time, go off with a hideous jangle.

We start to run for it. I hear Lizard whisper to Engelbrecht:

'Quick, put her hands back so she can't strike!' But it's too late. Miss Cuckoo Clock strikes midnight. And instead of a Cuckoo, a dear little carved Swiss cuckoo, there's a harsh whirr and a great bird of prey, something midway between a vulture and pterodactyl, dashes out at us. It does for Badger Norridge, severely prangs Lizard Bayliss, and the last we see of it is heading north with Engelbrecht in its beak.

We make our way back to the boat sadder and not much wiser men with nothing to show for our losses except an outsize cuckoo clock.

But who should greet us when we get back to the Club but Engelbrecht. It seems he overpowered his captor in mid-air and wrung its neck. The chef is even now cooking it for the wedding breakfast.

When, however, we remove Miss Cuckoo Clock from her travelling case, we find that marriage is absolutely out of the question. She is hopelessly fast and Dr Sadismus has to send her to the excitable ward of the Clock Hospital. On which rather sad note I must close the story of Engelbrecht's elopement.

# 13

# THEY WRESTLED ALL NIGHT

*". . . a mass of thrashing tentacles . . ."*

THE DECISION of my friend, Engelbrecht, the dwarf surrealist boxer, to hazard his tiny person in a season of All-in Wrestling, is not taken lightly.

I well remember the preliminary discussion that rages in the Screaming Room of the Surrealist Sportsman's Club. It is precipitated by a leading article in *The Fly-Paper* complaining of the decline of surrealist boxing, the occasion for which is the dreadful fiasco of the fight between Nitzy Nusselbaum and the Mighty Atomiser.

Nitzy Nusselbaum, you should know, is a nonogenarian cripple with such a complicated surgical history that it's whispered in the Dressing Rooms that when he goes to bed at night he unscrews his navel and his bottom drops off. As for the Mighty Atomiser, its reputation as a Tanker is so well known that its appearance in any ring is the signal for a massed chorus of *Rockabye Baby*. Neither of them would have got a licence if it hadn't been for Chippy de Zoëte straightening out the board of control. The resulting set-up bears, as *The Fly-Paper*'s boxing critic points out, about as much resemblance to a fight as a *marriage blanc*. Nitzy wins on points – points of etiquette, if you ask me; Chippy de Zoëte, who has been plunging heavily with all the borrowed time he can lay hands on, cleans up a packet, and everyone says this rings the death knell of surrealist boxing.

But when I turn to congratulate Engelbrecht, who retired undefeated champion way back, on having no more to do with the decadent sport, the gallant dwarf glares at me and grunts.

I observe that he is looking dangerously senile, and am all the more dismayed when I learn from his trusty but pessimistic manager, Lizard Bayliss, that he is meditating a come-back.

It appears that the up-keep of Engelbrecht's fiancé, Miss Cuckoo Clock, in the private mental ward of the Clock Hospital (Medical Supetintendent: Dr Sadismus) where she has been ticking away like an infuriated mob of death-watch beetles, ever since the night of her unfortunate elopement, has been making frightful inroads on my little friend's precious hoard of hours. Unless he can find some supplementary source of Duration he will be compelled, ere long, to keep an embarrassing and painful date with the Grim Reaper.

This, then, is the somewhat tricky background that has to be taken into consideration. Now you will understand why the tears are streaming down poor Lizard Bayliss's cheeks as he shakes his trembling head and piercingly flutes: 'So help me, kiddo, I never thought to see you clowning it in the mud bath with an electric eel, but if it's the only way we can foot our bills then what must be must.'

For all are agreed that, although boxing may be finished, and a come-back into the straight surrealist ring inadvisable, yet the jaded palates of the Fancy will find the psychopathological glamour of All-in Wrestling under the Salvador Dalí code irresistible.

The plan is simple enough. Engelbrecht is to be the star turn on a mammoth bill, promoted by Lizard Bayliss. What with the gate, which is expected to be astronomical, to say nothing of a few side bets, they reckon they ought to make a really big killing, enough to keep the dwarf out of the red for an indefinite Time to come.

There's a lot of organizing to be done, and, as usual, I find myself being pressed into service. My first job is to book suitable talent for the supporting bouts. Accompanied by my old cronies, Tommy Prenderghast and little Charlie Wapentake, I nip off on a lightning tour of the backblocks of Time and Space, to see what we can pick up.

I am watching, through a spy-hole, in the wall of a toughish little *boîte* called The Bottomless Pit, a promising free-for-all between Zombies and Giant Black Widow Spiders, when I receive a frantic message from Lizard Bayliss, summoning me back to Nightmare Abbey, where Engelbrecht is conducting his training in the ancestral swamp, by kind permission of his old friend and patron, the Id.

I find Lizard in tears as usual, shredding the gorse wig which we make him wear to prevent him tearing his hair out. 'Where's Engelbrecht?' I ask.

Lizard points to a fifty-foot anaconda which is coiled up on a bed of reeds, licking its lips. 'His sparring partner's just swallowed him,' he hiccoughs through his sobs.

'Come, come, Lizard,' I tell him. 'Pull yourself together, boy. This is no time to give way. We must get him out of there before he's digested. Have you tried an emetic?'

He nods glumly.

'Then we must shoot the brute.'

Lizard shakes his head. 'Can't do that. Might hit the dwarf or crush him in the convulsions. Beside, we need the snake on the bill.'

'If I were you,' says a reedy voice behind us, 'instead of standing there ringing my hands I'd ring a bell.'

We turn round and see the wraith-like form of the Oldest Member of the Surrealist Sporting Club, supporting himself on a forest of shooting sticks.

'Ring a bell,' he repeats solemnly, 'and the snake will think the round has come to an end and regurgitate its opponent.'

We do ring a bell, and with the precision of a trained all-in wrestler the anaconda disgorges Engelbrecht. It appears it never meant any harm. The holds they were rehearsing in that particular round were so tricky that it just got confused.

After a bath and a rub down the dwarf is as fresh as a daisy again. I report progress from my talent-spotting tour and we go into committee over the details of the billing. There is any amount of fixing and framing to be done and it's got to be totally hush-hush because if Chippy de Zoëte gets wind of it the odds will be all at sea.

Engelbrecht, however, with typical sportsmanship, is more intent on giving the public a really first-rate show than on making sure that his set-ups are water-tight...

Comes the big night and the vast Sportsdrome round behind the gasworks is crammed to extinction. The queues are so long that some of those who began lining up when they were quite young are qualified for the old age pension by the time they get abreast of the box office. Chippy de Zoëte's ticket spivs are doing a roaring trade.

At last the band of the Asylum Workers Union, ably conducted by Bandmaster Bulimia, which have been playing the *Paranoiacs' Polka* for as long as anyone can remember, switch over to that old favourite, *The Black Waltz*. The lights die away and the whole of that limitless arena is in darkness except for the spot playing over the twisted form of Crabs

From William Blake's Burning Book of All-in Wrestling
*Original in the Id's Gallery of Surrealist Sporting Pictures*

Felkin, our MC, who announces the bouts, and introduces Dreamy Dan, the surrealist referee.

I must say we certainly have done the fund proud. It's a bill to make your mouth water. First comes a little Free for All or Battle Royal between a dozen selected characters from English History: Strongbow, The Black Prince, John of Gaunt, Og, Gog, and Magog, Burke and Hare, Charlie Peace, Lord Roberts, and the Little Princes in the Tower.

There follows as close a spell of gouging and twisting as you could wish to witness. To those unacquainted with the elements of surrealist sporting set-ups, the cunning behind this selection may need a little emphasis. It is obvious that on form neither of the Little P's in the T stands an earthly. Ergo, argue the surrealist bookmakers, it's been fixed for one of them to win. But which one? Ah, that's not so easy. And so Engelbrecht's mob, who alone are in the know, get evens about a dead cert.

It's a pretty gory set-up, the way they play it. I won't bore you with the details. The heavy mob cancel each other out, as arranged. Then Burke knackers Hare and Charlie Peace coshes Burke. Lord Roberts, with a surprising turn of speed, whips off his cholera belt and garrottes Charlie Peace with it. The Little P's in the T gang up on poor old Bobs and do him brown. Then they pummel each other to a standstill. Dreamy Dan raises the hand of little Prince Edward and we score our first victory over the book.

Next comes a needle match if ever there was one. A five-round grapple between Jack the Ripper and Lucy, Lady Houston. For this ploy we are essaying a double bluff. On form Jack's got it in the bag. Ergo, argue the bookies, it's been fixed for Lucy and Jack is due to take a dive. So Lucy starts a firm favourite at three to one on. Moreover we arrange for her to receive Chippy de Zoëte in her dressing room, hung with Union Jacks, and she tells him she is confident of victory and tips him off that that nice Mr Engelbrecht will never allow that horrid Mr

Ripper to win. So Chippy de Zoëte puts everything he's got, including the Lady Houston Cold Cure, which she has kindly presented to him and which he wraps up in the tail of his shirt, on the old battleaxe at three to one on.

Meanwhile our mob has fixed for Jack to win after all and we stand to collect a packet.

But we have reckoned without Lucy, Lady Houston. When she comes into the ring in her Britannia outfit she gets a cheer such as you never heard, and Jack the Ripper, all in black, is booed nigh unto death. This goes to Lucy's never overstrong head. She forgets about her contract and goes all out for a win.

When Jack comes out of his corner for the first round, taking it easy so as to let the old girl toss him over her shoulder into the mud a few times, she pulls a hatpin on him, and the next thing we know his black shape is heading for dreamland as fast as thought. The only thing Dreamy Dan can do is to give Lucy the bout and when we've counted up our losses we're a long way behind what we had when we started.

Nor is this the only one that comes unstuck. A friendly five-round grapple between Salvador Dalí and a Haunted Case of Surgical Instruments – one of Tommy Prenderghast's discoveries – is thought to be such a dead cert in favour of the

inanimate objects that Engelbrecht hasn't even bothered to frame it. Despite the odds of 'Fifty to one on the bloodstained carving knives', which the surrealist bookies are calling hoarsely, we decide to plunge heavily in the hope of recouping ourselves.

At first all goes according to form. Midway through the third session Dalí is stretched out flat on the operating table, awaiting the autopsy. The crowd are singing, 'Good night, Salvador, see you in the next world!' The bookies are opening their calendars, clocks, and hour glasses, preparatory to paying out. But we have all of us reckoned without the Catalan sportsman's indomitable fighting spirit. Just how he wriggles out of the hold those bulldog forceps have got on him we cannot quite see, but there is no doubt it is one of the most spectacular come-backs in the history of All-in.

There is worse to come when the Invisible Man throws Jack Doyle, on whom we have our shirt. In the post-mortem that follows this upset it transpires that little Charlie Wapentake has omitted to give the Invisible Man his instructions. Asked why, he says, 'I couldn't find him so I assumed he wasn't there.'

What with all these disasters, by the time we arrive at the interval, before the main event of the evening, Engelbrecht has lost nearly all the profits on the takings, and is looking, as Lizard Bayliss remarks, so horribly old that anyone'd think it a kindness to send him to the vet in a cardboard box to have him put out of his misery.

We are in some confusion about our tactics. It had been our intention for Engelbrecht to win all his bouts except *the last*, and bets had already been placed with this end in view. But now we have grave doubts as to whether our champion can stand up against a packet of pins. There's only one thing for it and that is to give him a Time-transfusion. We call for volunteers and everybody whips out his calendar. By the end of the operation most of us are looking mighty doddery and all that remains of one or two are wigs and spectacles; but

it's a pleasure to see little Engelbrecht restored to his pristine state of vigour. Presently the siren sounds and we file out of the Changing Room and emerge at the ringside.

The first three bouts are treated more as exhibitions than anything else, and the bookies aren't taking any bets on them. Engelbrecht is in smashing form. He throws the Flying Scotsman out of the ring and gets a toe-hold on Moby Dick in no time.

He then proceeds to wrestle against an assortment of frightful phantasms of the unconscious, skeletons from the well-stocked cupboards of Nightmare Abbey, who appear by courtesy of the Id.

All this is just a little bit of limbering up preparatory to his main bout of the programme against the Great Kraken.

The giant cuttlefish is wheeled in in a tank. It clasps its sixty-foot tentacles above its head in acknowledgement of the plaudits of the crowd. Crabs Felkin introduces the contestants and we observe that Engelbrecht is wearing a frogman's suit. Obviously he intends to carry the fight to his opponent. Nor has he long to wait. Scarcely has Dreamy Dan pronounced the dread word: Time! than a tentacle flows over the edge of the tank, coils round Engelbrecht's ankle and drags him into the water. He goes down bubbling.

You would never think, to see that mass of thrashing tentacles and semi-ingested dwarf that the fight has been carefully rehearsed. We've even fitted the Kraken with an artificial scream that sounds under water at suitable moments, when the struggle seems particularly grim, for instance, when Engelbrecht is butting him in one of his giant eyes.

Backwards and forwards the battle rages. Once Engelbrecht manages to get a lock on the Kraken's beak; once he succeeds in throwing it right out of the tank but the tireless monster scrambles back into its home ground again, dragging with it not only the plucky dwarf, but also the occupants of half the ringside seats.

It really is an awe-inspiring spectacle and the crowd are in hysterics. The odds when it starts are two to one on Engelbrecht; because it's never occurred to any of the bookies that he'd drop the bout to a Cephalopod; but by the end of the fourth session the performance of both contestants has been so convincing that they've shortened to evens.

But in the fifth round something very unfortunate happens. The Kraken lets out a jet-black cloud of ink, which is direct violation of its contract. We see no more of Engelbrecht until he climbs out of the tank at the end of the round, black in the face, black all over, and fuming. 'So help me, I'll do that ruddy Cephalopod if it's the last thing I do,' he says. 'He fouled me with his beak under cover of that ink cloud.'

We try to restrain him but he won't listen. He clambers back into that tank and disappears into the black water, just like our old Saxon hero, Beowulf, going into the mere after Grendel's mother.

You can't see a thing because of the ink and the crowd are beginning to beef for their money back. Crabs Felkin tries to pacify them. 'Things,' he says, 'dear things, the grapple that's going on in that tank is so horrible that we've had to darken the water lest the sight of it should send you out of your wits. Dreamy Dan, our referee, who is right in there seeing fair play, has just sent a message out to say that he doesn't think he can stand a moment more of it.'

This, of course, is no way to pacify a surrealist sporting crowd, as Crabs should well know, and there is an ugly demonstration. Some of them try to rush the tank hut the Kraken whips out two tentacles and pulls them in, and all is comparatively quiet again.

Time rolls by, and the surface of that awful black water continues to be monstrously agitated by the death struggle going on in its depths. The Kraken's scream rings out loud and clear and goes on ringing. Lizard Bayliss looks worried. 'Do you think,' he says, 'that the dwarf's lost his head and is really doin' 'im? If he is, we're up the spout.'

Suddenly there is a fearful crash. A crack appears in the side of the tank. The inky water bursts through and floods the arena. When it subsides we see Engelbrecht sitting on top of the Kraken with his arms folded. He has tied the monster's tentacles into an inextricable knot; the giant Cephalopod is paralysed.

'That's torn it,' says Lizard Bayliss.

But we have reckoned without Dreamy Dan, our resourceful surrealist referee. He steps up to the Kraken, and with a mighty effort raises the tip of its smallest tentacle. 'The Cephalopod is the winner on a foul,' he announces. 'Engelbrecht pinched him in the bag.'

There is a howl of rage from the surrealist bookmakers, but there is no appealing against a referee's decision.

And so, despite his rash obstinacy, Engelbrecht's fortunes are retrieved.

Soon afterwards Dreamy Dan disappears and is never seen or heard of again, so we put up a memorial to him in the Liars' Room at the Surrealist Sportsman's Club.

# 14

# ENGELBRECHT UP!

*". . . the flames rise after them . . ."*

OF ALL the strange and stirring events in the Surrealist Sporting Calendar, none is so perilous, or so productive of casualties, as the historic steeplechase known, colloquially, as the Grand Cosmological. The going is so severe, the fences so stupendous, the water-jumps so extensive – to say nothing of other obstacles too horrible to mention – that only a thoroughbred Nightmare is likely to have any chance of finishing the course.

It is, therefore, with no little alarm and concern that I learn that Engelbrecht, the dwarf surrealist boxer, has not only entered a steed in the chase, but insists on riding it himself.

'Gone out of his tiny mind at last, if you ask me,' says Lizard Bayliss, my friend's trusty but pessimistic manager. 'Must be punch-drunk, after 'is scrap with the Witches' Pincushion. I can't stop 'im so I'll 'ave to start 'im. Come an' 'ave a decko at the "quadruped".'

We ascend to the Hippogriff Stables on the roof of the Surrealist Sportsman's Club and find Engelbrecht curry-combing a diminutive monster of the female sex, sound, obviously, in wind and limb, and a thoroughbred if ever I saw one, though, for a variety of reasons I should deem her unrideable, myself. She is tethered and hobbled so elaborately it reminds you of Houdini, and her wings have been docked to the bone.

'What's her name?' I enquire.

'Need you ask,' snaps Engelbrecht, nimbly dodging a massed attack from the serpents that compose the monster's mane. 'Medusa, of course.'

''E's 'ad to go to the Pasteur Institute three times already for inoculations of anti-venine serum,' says Lizard Bayliss sadly, waving a hypodermic syringe. ''E'll be bitten to death long before 'e reaches the first fence.'

I ask where Engelbrecht had got her.

Lizard Bayliss groans. 'Chippy de Zoëte put him on to her,' he says. 'Can you beat that, now? Chippy de Zoëte, the most unscrupulous nightmare-coper in the 'ole ruddy ring. Kidded 'im up with some yarn about 'er 'avin' belonged to an ancient Irish alcoholic paranoiac what 'ad 'ad the finest stable of Nightmares in the 'istory of psychiatry and 'ow she was goin' cheap on account of 'er mane. Cheap indeed! She'll cost 'im 'is ruddy life.'

'That be damned for a tale,' said Engelbrecht, who, with his usual adaptability is already affecting what he thinks is a suitably horsey style of talk. 'She's the finest little lepper in the barony is my Nightmare Medusa. And she's goin' to bring home the bacon, aren't you, my pretty? Whoa there, Medusa, steady girl! God-damn it, those ruddy adders have got me again! Quick, Lizard, the hypodermic. Inject me, pal, 'ere I swoon.'

Lizard gives him a shot of anti-venine and he goes on with his curry-combing, as cool as if Medusa was a Shetland pony.

Nobody takes Engelbrecht's entry seriously and the Surrealist Bookmakers are quoting Medusa a very long price.

'No student of form, however scrupulous,' writes Argus, the Racing Correspondent of *The Fly-Paper*, 'will be able to dismiss lightly, in a race of this peculiarly hazardous character, the possibility of a victory by a rank outsider, but there are several entries to which not even the most eclectic punter will – assuming, of course, that he is in his right mind – devote an instant's thought.' …He goes on to list a whole string of steeds finishing up with, 'The egregious Medusa, ridden (*sic*) by a totally inexperienced jockey, on whom I would not even venture the tail of my shirt, and, as you know, I take a pretty small size.' He adds that he has it on reliable information that the International Man-Hunt Committee, which is the governing body of Surrealist Steeplechasing, will refuse Engelbrecht a licence.

This so incenses the dwarf that he brings an action for criminal libel against the Editor of *The Fly-Paper*.

The membership of the Surrealist Sportsman's Club are present in force at the Id's annual house party at Nightmare Abbey for the race. Engelbrecht is subjected to showers of chaff; which doesn't improve his temper any.

After dinner, there is the time-honoured ceremony of spotting the winner. The Id's Grandmother, who has something of a reputation as a tipster, is wheeled in with her Witch Ball, by Lamia Lobb, the housekeeper. After a shot of hashish with a double mescaline as a chaser, she comes out of her coma with a crash and starts to tip.

'I see,' she says in her crackling voice that sounds like a second-hand furniture dealer feeling a lampshade, 'I see a chasm, measureless to man and wreathed in mist, through which peer evil shapes with clutching appendages. They are dragging the riders from their steeds…'

'She's tuned in to the water jump, all right,' says Charlie Wapentake. 'Stick to it, Granny! What else do you see?'

'I see an abyss of fire,' cackles the crone, 'with riders falling into it nineteen to the dozen.'

Charlie nudges me. 'That's Growlers' Gulf. Come on now, Granny. Tip us the winner!'

'I see,' continues the Id's Grandmother, 'a river of death over which one lone tiny rider is urging on his winged steed… He looks very small in the far distance…His colours are…'

But at that moment, just before she can give them her nap, the Witch Ball bursts, and the old lady refuses to say another word. There's a lot of discussion about the significance of the lone tiny rider, but, as Dr Sadismus points out, Lilliputian hallucinations, in which the subject sees brightly coloured scenes peopled with tiny little figures, are a common effect of mescaline, and most of the fancy remain sceptical. Nevertheless, such is the power of superstition, that several sportsman decide to have something on Engelbrecht, just in case.

As I accompany the dwarf up the winding staircase to his room in the tower he is muttering to himself: 'Curse that old crone! She'll shorten the odds with her cackle.'

'But surely,' I say, 'you've backed yourself ante-post?'

He shakes his head. 'Too risky. Have to take SP. Can't be certain of getting Medusa to the starting gate.'

'Well,' I says consolingly, 'I think you'll still get pretty long odds.'

And indeed, when we arrive at last at the tower it looks as if no odds could ever be long enough. The room, which

Engelbrecht is sharing with his manager and his Medusa, is empty save for Lizard Bayliss, who is in a stupor.

'Don't blame me, kiddo, if she's bolted,' he says when we revive him. 'She was tethered to the night-stool, double-nobbled hind and fore, an' munchin' 'er nose-bag of mandrake roots, as quiet as any Christian horse. Lamia Lobb comes up with a tasty dish of efts for me supper, and we chew the fat for a bit. Then I settles down for me night watch, and the next thing I know is you two bendin' over me. If you ask me I been slipped a Mickey Finn. Either that or them efts was out of season.'

'No doubt of it,' said Engelbrecht, a trifle bitterly, 'somebody slipped a dose of poppy in your mandragon.'

Lizard Bayliss says philosophically that perhaps it's just as well. Now there's no cause for Engelbrecht to go breaking his neck. But the indomitable dwarf isn't having any of that. He routs out Charlie Wapentake, whom he thinks he can trust, and they go and wake the Id's Grandmother, which is a pretty nasty thing to have to do.

The Id's Grandmother says she can't, of course, give them any definite info as her Witch Ball's bust, but from her long experience of the neighbourhood she's pretty sure that a stray hippogriff is bound to make for Witches Wen where it will be found cropping the Cronesbane, which is especially succulent just there.

It's a tidy step to Witches Wen, over very rough country, and when we do come up on Medusa, Lizard Bayliss is breathing like a horse with a tube in its throat, and before we can hobble her and slip the nooses, which Engelbrecht has borrowed from the curator of the Reptile House, over the vipers on her mane, she's airborne. However, it seems that Engelbrecht is the local Witches' nap. They've all put their broomsticks on his mount. So as soon as we explain the situation they nip off after Medusa and tether her to the top of a giant Deadwood Tree. Engelbrecht changes into his jockey's cap and silks, shins up the tree, and mounts her. He's not taking any more chances.

THE morning of the great race dawns dark and menacing, with the air all roaring with wind. Driving in the Id's vast barouche, up the dizzily precipitous track to the grandstand, we encounter a black vortex of bats, dislodged from the Church Tower by the tornado, and are nearly swept into the abyss. Nodder Fothergill, who is booked to ride one of the griffins from the Nightmare stable, shudders and huddles deep into his ulster. 'It looks,' he stammers between chattering teeth, 'as if the going's going to be a trifle rough.'

Nevertheless, despite the inclement weather, the paddock presents a scene of lively animation. The Surrealist Bookmakers are intoning the odds in their curious flute-like tones, with a dying fall on the penultimate syllable. Pegasus with Bellerephon up is, of course, the favourite, at 333–1. Then comes Mahomet's Burak, trained and ridden by the prophet himself. Also much fancied among the historical entries are Alexander's Bucephalus, Attila's Mongolian pony, Wok, which can run up any obstacle like a rat, and down the other side. Less heavily backed, because of his jockey's precarious seat, is a Ukrainian Tatar animal ridden by Mazeppa. Our olde English entries, Black Bess with Dick Turpin in the saddle, and Tom Pearce's Grey Mare, get a big hand from the sporting crowd; the chances of the latter, handicapped as she is by top-weight of jockeys are not very highly thought of.

The entries from the Nightmare Abbey stable, in addition to Nodder Fothergill's griffin, include the Devil's Dam, a gigantic black mare, unpopular with the field owing to her trick of snorting out great jets of flame from her nostrils. She is ridden by Wally Warlock, and it's all he can do to keep her under control; every time she turns her head she scorches the toe of his boots. Bones Barlow and Rollo Chatteridge, the joint masters of the Man-Hunt, are having a bit of trouble with their

Centaurs, Cheiron and Pholus. These, usually so well behaved, have made a bolt for the bar and are downing doubles in defiance of their jockeys. They can usually be relied on for a tip, so I stroll over and stand them each another double.

'Please don't give our Centaurs any more drink,' snap Bones Barlow and Rollo Chatteridge. 'They're half seas over as it is. They'll never be able to clear the first fence.'

'Nark it,' says Pholus. 'We need a few to steady our nerves if we're going to get round the course in weather like this. Any more out of you and we'll throw you.'

I stand them another and ask them if they know anything good. 'Well,' whispers Cheiron, 'whatever you do, don't back us because we're not trying.'

I remark that in view of his flying record Burak requires serious consideration.

Pholus shakes his head. 'I wouldn't put a trouser button on him if I were you. That aerial gallop of his isn't in the form book, you know. It's just a fanny spun by the Arab stable boys. Besides, if what we hear is true, the Prophet's due for another fit. They been and hocussed his sherbet. If I was you I'd keep me shirt tucked in tight.'

'You don't think Engelbrecht stands a chance on Medusa?' Lizard Bayliss enquires.

Pholus clears his throat and delicately wipes his mouth on his off fore hoof, but at that moment Dreamy Dan, our Surrealist Starter, trots past on his Eohippus, Crony, ringing his handbell for the weigh-in.

There are still no signs of Medusa or her jockey, and the Id and his friends are beginning to pass some very nasty remarks, when I catch sight of a cloud of witches flying low down over the grandstands. They fan out and in the middle of them is Medusa, with Engelbrecht still up.

'Engelbrecht,' says Dreamy Dan, 'you can't ride in this race if you're going to be piloted by a coven of witches. Either you run alone or I disqualify you.'

'That's all right, Dreamy,' says Engelbrecht, 'they're only my backers. None of them will be leaving the ground, because they're all putting their broomsticks on me.'

While they're weighing in Lizard Bayliss takes the witches round to the Surrealist Tote, where you can place a bet in anything, but literally anything, and they all put their broomsticks on Medusa.

'Oo-er,' says Lizard, when he rejoins me on the grandstand, 'I don't like this one little bit, chum. You know what those witches threaten to do if the dwarf don't win.'

It takes Dreamy Dan all the tact he can muster to get them lined up for a start, but at this point I think I'd better hand you over to little Charlie Wapentake who is in charge of the running commentary for the STT (Surrealist Telepathic Transference, guaranteed free from Delusions and Hallucinations).

' – Well, Things, here we are now, all ready for the start of this great race, and this is Charlie Wapentake giving you the commentary. Dreamy Dan, the Surrealist Starter, is lining 'em up. I think they're going to go. No, Lady Godiva, on Dobbin O'Coventry, is having trouble with her hair. This wind's very strong, you know. Ah, she's borrowed a hair-pin from one of the Valkyries. Now then...No, there's something wrong right out at the end of the line...Yes, Mazeppa's lodged a complaint against Engelbrecht's horse, Medusa. He says she's savaging him with her mane. Dreamy Dan's moved Engelbrecht further out. They're off any moment now. No they're not. There's a bit of bother in the centre. It's Squire Mytton on his pig, Fancy. He's objecting to Lord Raglan's Cavalry Sabre. And Uncle Tom Cobbleigh says Dick Turpin's had his watch. Dreamy Dan's losing patience...Ah, they're off at last.

'A bit ragged, but it'll do for a start. After all this is a pretty long course. Black Bess has taken the lead and Dick Turpin's sending her along as if the Bow Street runners were after

LADY GODIVA'S LAST RIDE

After William Etty, RA

Photo-finish to the Grand Cosmopolitan won by Medusa (Englebrecht up) from Dobbin O'Coventry (Lady Godiva up)

*Original in the Id's Gallery of Surrealist Sporting Pictures*

him. He'll never be able to keep that up. Ukrainian Tatar with Mazeppa up is close on his heels; Gad what a rotten seat that chap's got. Then comes Baron de Marbot,* but he keeps on turning his head to look at Lady Godiva. He'll be off if he's not careful. The rest of the field are all bunched together. And away they go hell for leather down the boulder-strewn, bog-rotten stretch to the first fence.

'And now, as all the runners have been swallowed up by a dense black cloud, I'm taking you over to Argus, the racing correspondent of *The Fly-Paper*, who's going to give you a running commentary from fence to fence all the way round. Over then to Argus.'

'Argus here: For those of you who aren't familiar with the course I'd better say a word about the first fence. It's nothing compared to some of the other obstacles, a mere Spanish convent wall with a revolving *cheval de frise* on top, the kind of thing that Don Juan Tenorio wouldn't even have needed a horse for. Here comes the first of them now. It's Black Bess. Turpin puts her straight at it and she takes it like a balloon. A lovely leap, and strictly in accordance with Man-Hunt Rules, which state that hippogriffs, ghost-horses and nightmares can only become airborne at obstacles. Otherwise they're disqualified...

'Some more have just gone over...Pegasus and Bucephalus, taking it very easy. Here comes Burak. I don't like the look of him much. He's blowing hard. And I don't like the look of his

* *The most dashing of Napoleon's Cavalry Officers.*

jockey, the Prophet, at all; he's rolling his eyes in a hopelessly crazy way. What's this? Lord Raglan and Baron de Marbot have stopped to fight a duel. I understand his Lordship objected to a remark of the Baron's about Lady Godiva, something to do with the wind in her tresses. Here come the ladies now, altogether in a bunch. Godiva on Dobbin O'Coventry. Brunhilde on Grane, with the Valkyries riding all round her, and a Unicorn ridden by a Virgin whose name I can't quite make out. And with them is little Engelbrecht on Medusa. Fancy letting yourself be piloted by Lady Godiva and a pack of Valkyries...His friends'll never let him hear the last of this...Well, I must hurry on to the next obstacle...

'Here we are now at the second fence, which is much more like an obstacle. It's a gigantic gallows with a revolving *cheval de frise* on top, and a row of hangmen waiting for you on a platform half-way down. I'm afraid it's proving too much for poor Turpin. He rises in his stirrups and gives a view halloa as he puts Bess at it. She's as game as they come but you can't jump over your fate. Yes, I thought so. The hangmen have got him. Well that's goodbye to another of our English entries...

'Here we are now at the first of the Water Jumps. The approach to it necessitates a very tricky bit of riding, through the ghoul-haunted woodland of Weir. There'll be a few casualties there, I'm afraid. They're thinning out now. Pegasus and Bucephalus are still leading but, damme, who's this? Squire Mytton on his wonder-pig, Fancy. Who said Britain was out of the race? Well run, Fancy. I never thought to see you stay so long. And look who's next. Tom Pearce's Grey Mare! with all six jockeys still up. No they're not. Harry Hawke's down, slipped over her tail just after the take-off. And he's brought Grane and the Valkyries down with him. Brunhilde tries to make Grane swim for it, but the water's hopping with Nibelungs and Grane's not having any. Here's Dobbin O' Coventry and Medusa. More mane trouble I expect. Engelbrecht's bright green and swollen up to twice his natural size; you'd have thought he'd have been immune to snake bite after all the practice he's had. I hear her Ladyship ask him:

' "I suppose you couldn't possibly lend me a hairpin, Mr Engelbrecht?"

' "Would a forked stick be any use, Mam?" says Engelbrecht.

' "Not much," says she, "seeing as how my hair is not composed of snakes, but thanks all the same."

'And up they go and over the dark water…'

'This is Argus again, giving you a running commentary of the race for the Grand Cosmological. I'm taking up my stand just in front of the historic Growler's Gull, the dread Abyss so called because Capt Growler, the pioneer Surrealist Jockey, disappeared into it the first time the race was run. A good many more will disappear into it this afternoon, and there's smoke and flames coming out in clouds. Here comes the field now, all bunched together. They're taking off now, and as they rise in the air the flames rise after them. The Prophet's turban's alight; he's off. Attila's on top of him. Crikey, what a spill! And Mazeppa's come untied at last. I daresay he's glad to be out of it. It's still anybody's race. Pegasus and Bucephalus are still flying neck and neck, a couple of lengths in front. Oh dear, there goes Squire Mytton down in flames; no doubt his breath caught alight; poor Fancy. Here comes Lady Godiva. She's flying it very high; doesn't want to get singed, I suppose. Medusa, on the other hand, is taking a dangerously low line. I think Engelbrecht hopes to shrivel up those snakes. I must say that dwarf's got pluck. Medusa's on fire! No, she's not, Engelbrecht's beaten out her mane. But he's lost an awful lot of ground…

'I'm taking you over now to the last water jump. It's a tributary of the Lethe and if you so much as splash yourself it's fatal. There's Old Charon in his boat, waiting to pick up any casualties and ferry them down into the main stream. And, by jove, he's got a pair of passengers now all right! The Greeks are out of the race. They were riding neck and neck as usual and Bucephalus suddenly started to savage Pegasus; the two hero-jockeys exchanged words and slashed at each other with their whips and before you could say Gyges they're both in the splash…

'Now it's between two of the rankest outsiders in the field. Lady Godiva's Dobbin O'Coventry and Tom Pearce's Grey Mare, with only Peter Gurney and Tom Cobbleigh up, all her other jockeys having fallen off; I wonder whether that'll disqualify her. Peter and Tom aren't sitting her very steady; I'm afraid they've been at their flasks again. Oh dear! Tom Pearce's Grey Mare pecks badly on landing and Peter and Tom roll off.

'All Lady Godiva's got to do now is to stay on for the last fence and ride Dobbin O'Coventry…

'But who's this coming down through the clouds? Can it be? Yes, by Gad it's Medusa with Engelbrecht still up. He's looking pretty queer, though. I wonder if he's still alive. It won't count on a win if he's not. The Man-Hunt rules are very strict about that. Yes, he's moving. Well, I shall have to eat my words about Medusa. She's gaining on Old Dobbin O'Coventry…

'The last fence on the Grand Cosmic course is known as the Golden Gate. It's not only very high, but also very highly polished, so that from the moment you take off, until you land, you see yourself as you really are.

'This is too much for poor Lady Godiva. Her hair stands straight up on end. She screams so loud that old Dobbin O' Coventry falters.

'"Is anything the matter Mam?" says Engelbrecht, over his shoulder as he swings alongside.

'"You never saw such a sight as I look," says she.

'"Well, if my cap's any use to you, take it and welcome, Mam," says the courtly dwarf…

'They're over the Golden Gate now and coming in for the finish. Medusa's two lengths ahead. Godiva can't get an inch more out of Old Dobbin. Medusa passes the post. Medusa's the winner…'

Then we're taken back to Charlie Wapentake in the Grandstand who describes the scene when the Chief Witch leads in Medusa and Engelbrecht faints into Lizard Bayliss' arms and has to be rushed to the Pasteur Institute.

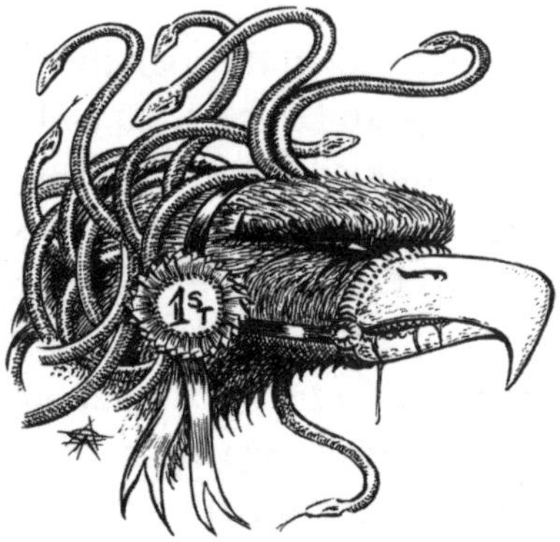

# 15

# A QUIET GAME OF CHESS

*". . . shooting down our Hangovers . . ."*

IT WAS THE Boxing-day after the last Christmas before the End of the World, and, together with a sizable handful of my fellow-members, I was lounging away the remaining shreds of the tattered epoch in the Trance Room of the Surrealist Sporting Club.

We were engaged in the traditional Boxing-day pastime of shooting down our Hangovers. Chippy de Zoëte, with a shrewd left and right from his trusty old elephant gun, had just put paid to a frightful fanged Apparition who had been pursuing him hotly ever since breakfast. Nodder Fothergill was taking aim at a great grey Cloud of Unknowing that hovered over the sofa on which he lay outstretched. Wally Warlock was blazing away at the Spots in front of his eyes. Engelbrecht, the dwarf surrealist boxer, had just brought the chandelier crashing to the floor and blown off several of the Oldest Member's members in a plucky but characteristically rash attempt to dispel by rocket-fire a hideous black Shape answering to the name of the Dark Night of the Soul which was harassing his trusty but congenitally melancholic old manager, Lizard Bayliss.

At that moment the Id, who had been shouting away to himself in the Silence Room, blew in and challenged all and sundry to a quiet game of chess.

I don't know whether you've ever played surrealist chess. It's a bit different from the ordinary kind. Not only does it include additional pieces such as the Tank, the Fighter Plane, and the Atomic Bomb which were introduced into the game by King Abdulla of Transjordania to bring it into line with modern power politics, but it is played with human Kings, Queens, Bishops, Knights, and Pawns, with genuine old machicolated castles for Rooks, all on a board of positively cosmic dimensions. So much so that the doors of the Surrealist Chess Stadium have proved before now to be the portals to several other worlds besides the next.

It was with some trepidation, therefore, that I accepted Engelbrecht's invitation to join the HQ staff of the scratch unit which he undertook to put on to the board against the task-force of Grand Masters fielded by the Id. And, as so often happens in Surrealist Sport, there was a powerful whiff of dirty work in the ether. I noticed that nearly all the Old Hands – clutchers, most of them, if you ask me – had enlisted on the side of the big battalions, and Chippy de Zoëte, always a tough and slippery customer, had been commissioned Pawn-Master.

Indeed, when our side assembled in the funereal dressing room – we had drawn Black, of course – we were reduced to Engelbrecht, Lizard Bayliss and myself, little Charlie Wapentake (as defective as he is devoted) and as much of the Oldest Member and his members as could be collected from the Club carpet.

'You haven't been betting, have you, kiddo?' Lizard Bayliss asked nervously as he adjusted his crêpe chess-helmet.

Engelbrecht nodded vigorously. 'You bet I have,' he said.

'Everything we possess. Everything I could think of. Plus all the Time we got left plus what we won from Grandfather Clock. Why not?' He hiccoughed and was immediately enveloped in a dense cloud of black smoke.

Plainly the fighting dwarf was still under the direct influence. He had not even begun to approach the Hangover stage.

Presently the professional umpire, Dreamy Dan, who umpires all surrealist sporting contests, wandered in to say it was time we were getting out on to the board as the pieces had arrived. We hurried out to look them over.

It was obvious that the Id had not been letting the grass grow under his feet. The Black pieces were the most moth-eaten collection of disintegrating old hams you ever set eyes on outside the waiting room of a theatrical agency. As for the pawns they were nothing but a gang of dead-end kids and I wasn't a bit surprised to find they were out on ticket of leave from an approved school.

White, on the other hand, was as well disciplined a set as any turned out by old man Staunton himself. They lined up in formation and marched off, chanting in unison the daring slogan: 'One, two, three, four! Pawn to Queen's Bishop Four.'

Then the umpire's helicopter became airborne and not long after the boom of the Sunset Gun announced the start of play.

The Oldest Member took a pinch of gunpowder from his snuffbox and passed the flame of his lighter under his nostrils. He appeared to benefit from the resulting explosion. It enabled him to take in the situation at a glance. 'The first thing to do,' he said, 'is to submit those pawns to a severe loyalty test.'

'Better save your strength,' said Lizard. 'Every piece we got's been got at, if you ask me. Might just as well line up

the whole lot on the fifth column, bump 'em off and call it a day.'

'You let me get at 'em,' said Engelbrecht, lurching forward. 'Listen to me, you spivs,' he roared. 'I don't care how often you've broken your old mothers' hearts or cheated the hangman. You're chessmen now, see. Black chessmen. And when I give the word I want you to get cracking into the middle of that board and knock hell outa them White bastards. Now…'

His voice was drowned in a ragged cheer. The Black King started to recite Henry V, and three pawns, fired by the general *élan*, dashed forward in a charge.

'Get back to your squares, you bloody little stoats,' yelled Charlie Wapentake.

We held an emergency conference. Night was falling. Only one thing was clear, which was that our Captain did not know the first thing about the Game. Lizard Bayliss, living in the world of fisticuffs where the higher cerebral sports are but little esteemed, had never graduated beyond the draughts-board, and could only mutter 'Huff him, chumbs, huff the bleeders to death!' Charlie Wapentake was still concussed as the result of having been fool's-mated so often at his prep school. My own chess-lore is rudimentary. It seemed we should have to rely on the Oldest Member's Memory.

From the White end of the board a rocket soared up into the night and burst releasing a cluster of incandescent stars which arranged themselves in the symbols PK4. The Id had moved.

Engelbrecht reeled up to our King's Pawn and aimed a savage kick at the child. 'Two squares forward! March!' he roared. Around midnight the KP got through on his Walkie Talkie Apparatus to say that K4 was untenable. I jumped into a staff car and shot off to investigate.

I must say the route to PK4 was a pretty gruelling one. The car sank under me in a bog near the frontier of K3 and K4 and I had to do the last part on foot. I found the pawn skulking about under a Upas tree. 'I don't like it 'ere, sir,' he whined. 'There's things, nasty things.' 'What of it,' I roared, 'there's nasty things everywhere. The Universe is stiff with 'em. You'll either do your duty and hold this square or be court-martialled and shot on the spot.' Just then there was a moaning gibbering noise and something in a white sheet flitted by. I took a pot-shot at it and heard a frightful but all too familiar curse. It was Chippy de Zoëte, trying some of his favourite psychological warfare tactics.

Shortly after I arrived back at HQ another rocket signal went up. The Id had castled on the King's side.

'Castled has he?' said Engelbrecht. 'Well we'll castle too. How do we do it?'

How indeed? For no sooner did we start to move our King's Rook than the entire structure collapsed in a shower of brick-dust and plaster, jackdaws' nests, and bats. We heard a thin voice somewhere in the middle of it all say: 'I'm very old and very tired.' And that was how a very gallant edifice passed over to the other side.

We called for volunteers to rig a temporary structure on KB1, put Lizard Bayliss inside it to make it stand up, and just managed to get the job done before the time signal went for us to move. But we had reckoned without the Id. When the King took up his position on KKt1 there was a violent explosion. While we had been busy reconstructing, enemy paratroops had mined the square. An attempt to take advantage of the confusion and kidnap the Queen was discovered in time by QP and QBP who heard the old girl holler and gave the alarm.

The preliminary phase of court intrigue was now over. The middle game, and with it all the horrors of mediæval warfare, had begun in earnest. Soon the board was one vast panorama of carnage. The screams of hapless pawns being dragged away to captivity with all its nameless horrors, the wheezy death rattle of knights, the whining supplications of crafty bishops, the sadistic frenzy of queens, resounded on all sides. It was too much for poor little Charlie Wapentake. He developed Chess-shock. 'I can't stand it,' he said, burying his face in his hands. 'I can't stand it I tell you. It's too horrible.'

'And what about me shut up in this here bloody tower,' said the hollow cardboard voice of Lizard Bayliss. Sternly we ordered him back to his square…

At dawn on the seventh day I returned to HQ weary and travel-stained after a long-distance recce up in the mountains at QR6 where one of our pawns, a boy scout type, had been making some progress. Engelbrecht was snoring on his camp bed. The Oldest Member was at the control panel. 'Let me put you in the picture,' he said. 'We've had a pretty severe pranging but I think we can say that our position is still defensible. We've got rid of the worst of our fifth column by process of exchange which is whizzo so far as it goes and we've held our own in pieces. But we're badly behind in tempo, and I'm afraid we shall feel it as soon as the secret weapons come into play. The purple's up already.'

LULL BETWEEN MOVES

A leaf from the sketch book of Official Surrealist War Artist Sir John Tenniel

*Now on view in the Surrealist War Museum*

Next moment Dreamy Dan's voice sounded on the loud speaker: 'Tank to Tank's twelfth, Check. And Flame Thrower to Flame Thrower's sixth, Double Check.'

'I expected as much,' the OM went on. 'Well, we must evacuate our King to safety. I've booked him a room at the Palace.'

The next twenty-four hours were hellish. We were attacked on all sides by newly invented pieces including bacteriological warfare units in flagrant defiance of the rules of all forms of chess. All appeals to Dreamy Dan were met with his invariable formula – accompanied by a schizophrenic chuckle – of: 'Can't say I noticed anything special. You must be seeing things.'

Our own shock-pieces proved, as we had feared, markedly inferior to the enemy. The Tank moved straight into a trap. The Fighter Plane was held immobilized by a Ray apparatus on Rocket Bomb's ninth…

The concrete bunker which was our HQ was given over to black despair, so black you could scarcely see your hand in front of your face. Our Atomic Bomb had been taken *en passant* before it had had a chance to go off. The White pieces were milling all round the Palace Hotel where our trusty old Monarch was sitting shivering in the Winter Garden humming *God Save the King* to keep his spirits up. 'It's Mate in two whatever we do,' said the Oldest Member. I had never seen Engelbrecht so downcast.

There was a scratch at the door and Lizard Bayliss poked his head round.

'What are you doing, Lizard?' I said. 'I thought you'd been taken years ago.'

'So I was,' said Lizard, 'but I escaped. Had a hell of a job to get across the board. I got a message for you. It's from the little bleeder of a pawn, you know the boy scout type what was so keen. You should see where he's got to. Way out behind their lines 'e is. 'E couldn't let you know before because Chippy de Zoëte smashed his Walkie Talkie App way back on QR3. 'Ere, read this. It's hot.' He handed over a crumpled note.

Engelbrecht read out: 'Have infiltrated to QR 666th disguised as brushwood stop Enemy's Atom Bomb *en prise* stop Chance of Mate in two stop Move me quick. Sgd QRP.'

The Oldest Member positively leapt to the controls. 'QRP takes Atom Bomb and Atom Bombs, Check!' he announced. 'It's Mate in two whatever they do.'

We heard over the intercom a shaky voice saying: 'White resigns!' But it was too late. The dizzy height of promotion from Queen's Rook's Pawn to Atom Bomb had gone to our little boy scout's head. 'I'm not accepting any resignations,' he squeaked, 'I detonate.'

Next moment there was a blinding flash and the Universe turned into a nebula.

'This,' said the Oldest Member, 'is where I came in.'

**THE END**

Maurice Richardson 1907—1978

# UNQUIET WEDDING

*". . . a civic ceremony and reception at the Albert Hall . . ."*

THE ANNOUNCEMENT that a marriage had been arranged and would shortly take place between Dracula's Daughter and the Son of Frankenstein was received in crime-fiction circles with general satisfaction.

It caused little surprise. The tendresse between the two young friends had been the subject of ghoulish gossip for some time. Indeed, the news of the engagement would have been released long before had it not been for the dispute between Count Dracula and Frankenstein Senior over the film rights of the first-born of the forthcoming alliance, and whether the new picture should be titled Dracula's Granddaughter or Grandson of Frankenstein.

In the Conference Room at Castle Dracula agreement had been reached at last, thanks to the arbitration of Professor Moriarty, as chairman of the Fiction Fiends' Guild. They went on to discuss details of the wedding. Frankenstein Senior, who suffered from delusions of grandeur, favoured

Westminster Abbey. It took time to explain to him that Vampires were not admitted. Finally they agreed on a civic ceremony and reception at the Albert Hall.

The last item on the agenda, No 637, was Guarding the Presents. Dracula thought this a trifle which could be safely left to the bride's relatives. But with an ejaculation like the rumble of traffic, Frankenstein registered dissent.

'Did I understand you to say you preferred defectives or–er detectives Herr Frankenstein?' Moriarty asked.

Thus it was that invitations to the Dracula Frankenstein wedding were sent to some three thousand detectives ranging from Sherlock Holmes to Val Fox, Joey the parrot, and Rin Tin Tin*.

'Surely, Holmes, you're not going to accept?'
'And why not, pray, Watson?'
'But it's a trap.'

---

**The author maintains that any serious detective story reader should recognise most of the characters that follow. Pass mark 30 out of the 36 listed on page 189.*

'On the contrary, I believe it to be a perfectly genuine invitation. As master of ceremonies at a wedding where an unprecedentedly large number of suspicious characters will be present, Moriarty is following the only logical course. Like any other man of rational mentality he calls in the expert.'

'Don't be such a blithering little idiot, Bunny. Of course we're going. Now just give my topper a brush like a good rabbit.'

'But, Raffles, it's madness! With three thousand detectives there we don't stand a chance.'

'My good Bunny, you surely don't think I'm such a cad as to wangle an invitation to a fashionable wedding and then pinch the presents? I'm not concerned with the swag at all. But our position in society demands that we should go. Everybody who is anybody will be there.'

'*Count Dracula requests the presence of Capt and Mrs Drummond at the marriage of his daughter, Lamia, to Mr. Frankenstein, Junior*...Never heard of 'em. Who's Lamia Dracula, Phyl? Is she some school pal of yours, little girl?'

'Don't ask me, precious. You know what my memory's been like ever since Irma Peterson gave my brain away to an ape. I expect we were finished together. Anyway it sounds an awfully smart do. That reminds me, idiot boy, I saw the most adorable hat yesterday, a complete model of Kew Gardens...'

'What do you think, Fosco? Lot of infernal humbug, eh? Out with it, man! No copybook morality, if you please!'

'Gently, my good Perceval, gently. We walk, as ever, upon egg shells. I would counsel both of you to put in an appearance, but in order to dispel unfortunate impressions first, please, to remove the handcuffs from Lady Glyde.'

'I'll see her damned first.'

'But, Dad, if Philo Vance and Nero Wolfe are going I've just got to be there.'

'Over my dead body, Ellery. No Queen ever attended a Vampire's wedding. I tell you, son, it ain't natural.'

'I believe you've got one of your premonitions, Poirot.'

'*Ma foi*, Hastings, but your perspicacity astonishes me. Yes, to use your quaint English expression, I sniff ze red herring at ze bottom of ze well.'

Out of consideration for the vampire element the ceremony was to begin an hour after lighting-up time. Long before then, the body of the hall had become obscured by the barrage of tobacco smoke rising from the pipes and cigarettes of the detectives. Outside a dense fog had been thickening steadily ever since breakfast. It was, as one wag put it, the most perfectly horrible weather imaginable.

The presents, some in glass cases, some on velvet plush stands, had been arranged in a towering pyramid in the centre of the hall. From his eyrie in the organ loft, Holmes surveyed the scene through a pair of night-glasses.

Wheezing from his climb, Inspector French poked his head round the corner of the loft. 'Excuse me, Mr Holmes,

but are you aware of the nature of the gifts?'

'I've been too busy organising their protection to be aware of anything. What are you insinuating, Inspector?'

French cleared his throat, and read aloud from his notebook: 'List of stolen articles observed among wedding presents at Albert Hall. The Ascot Gold Cup. The Portland Vase. Queen Marie Antoinette's Necklace. The Koh-i-noor Diamond. The Gutenberg Bible. The *Mona Lisa*. The Rokeby *Venus* . . . Shall I go on, sir? It's a very long list. In fact there's only one present that's not stolen, as far as I can see.'

'And what may that be?'

'A cricket bat inscribed 'from WG Grace to AI Raffles, in memory of Gentlemen vs Players, Lord's, 1895'.'

'Really, French, you put me in a deuced awkward position. We don't want to mar this festive occasion with the stigma of an arrest.'

'No sir. But neither the High Commissioner nor my author would approve of me guarding stolen property. As for Sir Arthur, God bless him, he'd turn in his grave. I've spoken to Inspector Lestrade and he's ever so cut up.'

'That's quite enough, French. Attend to your duties.'

The simple little ceremony took place on the stage. Those who were near enough to see through the smoke, noticed that the bridegroom was unable to write his name. A copy of his thumb-print was rushed to Scotland Yard. After kissing the Bride, the registrar turned white as a sheet and had to sit down.

Afterwards there were reunions all over the hall. Old friends and old fiends greeted each other uproariously through the murk and raised tankards of champagne and stout.

'How d'ye do, Clubfoot? How do, Nikola? Nice to see you looking so fit. Suppose it's those Tibetan prescriptions of yours. I always think an all-black wedding's awfully pretty, don't you, countess? Yes, ever so pretty. Dear me, how washed-out Lady Glyde's looking. And stumbling all over the place, poor thing. I never did think Blackwater was healthy. Wonder Sir Perceval doesn't get his drains seen to. Daren't, eh? Well perhaps not. Yes, I see what you mean. Case of letting sleeping wives lie? Hullo, there's Grimsby Roylott. Glad to see you've brought your little pet with you, Doctor! Anybody know where the young couple are going for their honeymoon? The Royal College of Surgeons Museum? You don't say! Still it'll be nice and quiet for them. Why, when I married the first Mrs Joseph Smith, we... What's that he's saying through that megaphone? Is there a doctor in the Hall? Hundreds of 'em I should think, but I'd be mighty careful which one I went to, eh Cream? Who's been taken ill, I wonder? The registrar? Sudden attack of pernicious anaemia? Now I wonder where he could have caught that from? Ha, ha, ha, ha, ha, ha.'

From the phalanx of detectives drawn up in circular formation round the tier of presents, came a confused babble of boasting and gossip. Especially vociferous were the younger school.

'So I told my author. I told him straight: if you don't sell the film rights of my next...But, good heavens, nobody uses clues and deduction these days. It's all done by feminine intuition, unless of course you're one of the toughies. Who said so? Holmes? You don't mean to say you pay any attention to that corny old ham! Why he's crusted, my dear, simply crusted with barnacles. And doped up to the eyes. They say he's going to Mrs Bradley to be analysed. Tell me is it true that Peter Wimsey's taking orders? I hear he's receiving instruction from Father Brown. I don't think you've any right to say that. After all your author only got a third in English. Oh look there! A fight! Lemmy Caution's knocked out Slim Callaghan, and Slim Callaghan's knocked out Lemmy Caution. Who's that comic period-piece over there whispering to Inspector French?'

'Inspector French? I have a message for you from Mr Sherlock Holmes. He says he has Professor Moriarty's personal assurance that the presents are all on loan and will be returned to their rightful owners after the close of the reception. The whole thing is just a little symbolic gesture. Do you understand?'

'No, doctor. I can't say I do.'

'Well, nor do I. But then I never did.'

'I say, Phyl, it's awflilly stuffy in here. Mind if I pop outside for a moment? My fingers are simply itching for the feel of a mashie niblick. Shan't be long. Just a quick pitch and putt with Algy in Kensington Gardens. Peter'll keep an eye on you. Won't you, Peter?'

'Of course, old boy…half a tick, Phyllis. I've just got to see a thing about a thong.'

'Phyllis! Darling!'

'Irma! Why it must be simply ages. I say, mind my eye with that cigarette holder. I like your Crook's New Look.'

'Tell me, sweetie, is that a golf course on your head? Because if it is I'd like to wend my way to the clubhouse and drop in at the nineteenth. Come on, angel, let's take our twigs to the girls' room, let our back hair down and have a real old hag's cackle…'

'But Irma, they've taken all the mirrors away!'

'Course they have, goosey. This is a Vampire's Party. Didn't you know?'

'Vampires! Oooher! And what's that trunk doing over there? Oh, Irma! You're not going to kidnap me again?'

'Watson! What was that frightful bellow just now?'

'I hardly like to tell you, Holmes, but I fear it was Drummond.'

'His usual trouble, eh? We are in deep waters, Watson. Wake Mycroft!'

'But I don't know what he's disguised as.'

'Professor Moriarty? I am the Transylvanian Ambassador. I bear a challenge from His Excellency, Count Dracula. His Excellency demands the satisfaction for your insult to his honour in inviting to his daughter's wedding his mortal enemy, Dr van Helsing.'

'But I assure you it was utterly unintentional. The invitations were sent out by my PRO, Col Sebastian Moran, here, to a list supplied by the Reading Room at the British Museum.'

'Under the Transylvanian Blood Code that makes no difference. You have choice of weapons, of course.'

'Go on, Professor. Don't be so chicken-livered. You can take my sporting Lee Metford.'

'What's the use of that against a Vampire, you fool?'

---

'But, my dear Captain Drummond, surely you are not seriously accusing Mr Vance of kidnapping your wife and holding her to ransom?'

'I certainly am! Why the man's a thorough decadent. Writes poetry. Studies Chinese Art. Shouldn't wonder if he wasn't on Fu Manchu's payroll. Now you keep out of this Holmes. Go and play trains at Baker Street Station. Algy! Peter! Denny! Carstairs! Carruthers! Come on Gang! Let's give the scum a loyalty test.'

'See here, Drummond, my name's Marlowe and this is my colleague, Sam Spade. We'd have you know that Mr Vance is not a client of ours, but we're not going to stand by and see an innocent American citizen beaten up this way even if he is a private detective.'

---

'May I introduce Mr Raffles – Mr Arsène Lupin?'

*'Enchanté cher confrère.'*

*'Moi aussi.* Er – *mon ami Lapin et moi penson*

*que*...er, what I mean to say is we think this job's a little too big for one firm...'

'But aren't you going to use an anaesthetic, gentlemen?'
'What! On Bulldog Drummond? No fear!'

'Now then, Bunny, look sharp with that torch! What's that you say? Your arm is held by a Gigantic Beetle?* Oh my poor Bunny, whatever have you been reading?'

'And so, you see, Mr Holmes, I find myself in as trying a predicament as any I have been in since the day you pushed me backwards over the Falls.'

'If it's any consolation to you, Professor, you have succeeded in ruining my reputation.'

'Dear me, Mr Holmes, dear me.'

'But that does not absolve you from your engagement of honour. Well, Watson? What is it?'

'Even the animals are at it now, Holmes. The Hound of the Baskervilles is mauling Rin Tin Tin, and Joey the Parrot's making the feathers fly from the Jackdaw of Rheims. If this goes on there won't be a single character left in crime fiction or history.'

'All that huge expanse of cerebral cortex, Professor, and not an idea to save the game? Yes, Watson? Have you something to say?'

'Holmes ! I've got it. The only way. We must send for an author.'

* The Great Beetle Mystery, *by Richard Marsh; an Edwardian occult thriller which was a best seller in its day.*

### IN 'UNQUIET WEDDING'...

Count Dracula and his bane, Dr Van Helsing, the Dutch vampirologist, appear by courtesy of the late Bram Stoker, Irving's manager, author of *Dracula*. Frankenstein is, of course, the name of the monster's proprietor, in Mary Shelley's story, but we have followed the incorrect modern practice. Moriarty only made one personal appearance, in *The Final Problem*, the last story in *The Memoirs of Sherlock Holmes*, but his presence is felt offstage in *The Valley of Fear*; Col Sebastian Moran, his right-hand man, appears in the first story in *The Return of Sherlock Holmes*. Detective Val Fox and his sagacious parrot, Joey, used to feature in a children's detective story series in the immortal *Rainbow*. Rin Tin Tin will be familiar to film-goers. Raffles and his Bunny, from the amateur cracks-man stories of Conan Doyle's brother-in-law Hornung, are almost as well known as Holmes and Watson. Lupin occurred in countless *Stories* by Maurice Leblanc. Sapper's *Bulldog Drummond* saga has provided Drummond, his Phyllis, and Irma Peterson and some of Drummond's gang. Count Fosco and Sir Perceval Glyde appear by courtesy of Wilkie Collins, author of *The Woman in White*. Philo Vance, SS van Dine's creation, was a famous American detective of the twenties, school of Holmes. Rex Stout's Nero Wolfe still flourishes; so do Ellery Queen's Ellery Queen and Agatha Christie's Poirot and Hastings, and Freeman Wills Croft's Inspector French. Valentine Williams' Clubfoot has been in retirement for some time. Dr Grimsby Roylott was the villain and proprietor of Doyle's *The Speckled Band*. Dr Nell Cream and Joseph Smith were both real murderers. Dr Nikola, that equivocal hero-fiend, we owe to Guy Boothby. Mrs Bradley is the property of Miss Gladys Mitchell. Lord Peter Wimsey belongs to Miss Dorothy Sayers; Father Brown to the late GK Chesterton; Caution and Callaghan to Peter Cheyney; Spade and Marlowe to Dashiel Hammett and Raymond Chandler respectively.

*MR*

# AFTERWORD

When *The Exploits of Engelbrecht* was reprinted, in a modest edition, by John Conquest in 1977, I bought a fair part of his run. I gave the book to strangers in the street, I sent it abroad to baffled Berliners and Bosnians, I pressed it upon all visitors. Many of whom appreciated the book and thanked me for it. Yet, in spite of all talking up, that printing vanished from the world as thoroughly as the first edition or the issues of *Lilliput* in which they first appeared. I've concluded therefore that no matter how many copies of *The Exploits of Engelbrecht* are printed, they will continue to vanish into oblivion as soon as they are published.

Some of us will have the chance to read them before they vanish again. Hold on to the copy you have here. It's the best edition you'll probably ever see, the product of genuine enthusiasm, of Savoy's old habit of putting their money where their mouths are, careless of financial reward and willing to spend uneconomic amounts to produce the best possible book they can. They know they'll never make money and publish books like this with their eyes wide open. If they break even, they believe they've had a success. You are getting very good value if you paid for this book.

Richardson's best work (and this is his best work) reflects the eclecticism as well as the attitudes of a barroom scholar of the finest type. The kind of man who when a colleague comes in with news that Nathalie Sarraute is suing Anaïs Nin for plagiarism pauses with drink to lips and murmurs 'How can she tell?'

Soho used to be loaded with the bastards. Some of them were, like Henry Williamson, fascist and superior novelist, famous for a thinking salmon, unexpected monuments. Robin Cook was another, at the French, dying before your eyes and telling stories faster than Ken Dodd. The great Secker editor, John Blackwell, was dry-witted straightman for many of the best. They'd tell you your stories. Their stories. His stories. Her stories. Raconteurs but not bores. Curious about everything and everyone. Telling stories to save their lives. Willing to try anything once and more than once if you don't remember trying it the first time. Able to produce the shortest, sparest amount of copy for the maximum available dosh, they could be relied upon for laconic wit, a touch of genius, no matter what they were writing. Kersh could do you two columns of rhyming couplets after a splash of cold water to his face and the promise of payment on delivery.

*Lilliput*, where Richardson was on the editorial team, was full of them. Jim Cawthorn lists some of them in his introduction. Fitzrovians with no homes to go to but the editorial office and the BBC. He, like me, knew a few of the others, in those last glorious years of Fleet Street when runners were employed to go from pub to pub looking for reliable copy-producers who were still sober enough to hit the keys of their typewriters.

Their ghosts mingle with Richardson's in the pubs and drinking clubs where literary men (and they are literary men) gather to tell one another stories. Jack Trevor Story. Gerald Kersh. Baker. Do you a thousand words on anything you like. Cash. There you go, George, wipe it off the slate and start again.

They're still at it somewhere, in a seedy basement barroom they call heaven. And they're gathering round Richardson because he remains one of the best. And they're buying him sweet gins and wishing they had written just one of the Engelbrecht stories. When he's gone – to the gents or back to the office, or wherever – they remember those stories and retell them. Stories of grandfather clock fights, witch hunts and plant theatres.

Richardson's an enthusiasm you share. You can judge your friends by what they think of him. You can judge your enemies, too. And Richardson knew all about judging enemies. The equanimity which informs his best fiction and sporting features could disappear as fast as Ronnie Kray's smile.

He had something of a quarrelsome nature, which was not the handicap it is for all of us, since he was also a trained fighter. He grew up in the days when you had to be good at some sport, preferably something violent. Even Bonfiglioli had his foils and sabres, his Webley. Kersh was a wrestler, fit and strong and able to sink thirty pints a night. Richardson was handy with his dukes and it's probably fair to say that Engelbrecht was in personality not entirely unlike his creator. Richardson had an odd brain. Having an odd brain turns quite a few people to the pleasures of drink. They hope the drink will make them banal and often it does. Richardson, by all accounts, could be a bit aggressive, a bit boorish on occasions, but mainly he had style. It needed a lot of sweet gin to make him boring. That style's embodied in these stories. Don't lose them. Don't take your eyes off them. Keep them safe. These are the accounts of the Surrealist Sporting Club. They are the work of a crafty master. They are jealously recovered, if not properly appreciated. Believe me, something happens to them. They have a habit of vanishing out of your hand. They leave your shelves without a trace, whispering off into that infinite night. They continue to exist, of course, malleable like Dalí watches, but probably disguised. I almost didn't appear in this book. If the cat hadn't found it, I would probably be somewhere else, in the wrong book altogether.

*Michael Moorcock*
*Circle Squared Ranch*
*Lost Pines*
*Texas, USA*

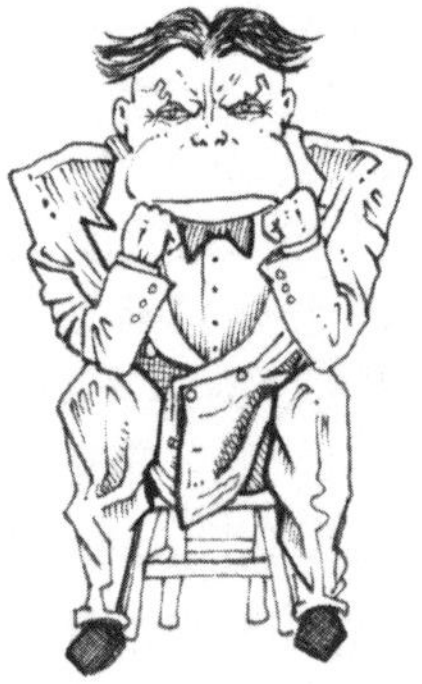

Lilliput
OCTOBER 1948
ONE SHILLING
Trier

Lilliput
MARCH 1949
ONE SHILLING
Trier

Lilliput
JULY 1949
ONE SHILLING
Trier

Lilliput
DECEMBER